THE
BRUZ

THE
BRUZ

DR. ARMONDO COLLINS

AuthorReputationPress®
Creativity & Branding

Author Reputation Press LLC
45 Dan Road Suite 5
Canton MA 02021
www.authorreputationpress.com
Hotline: 1(888) 821-0229
Fax: 1(508) 545-7580

Ordering Information:
Quantity sales. Special discounts are available on quantity purchases by corporations, associations, and others. For details, contact the publisher at the address above.

Printed in the United States of America.

ISBN-13:   Softcover   978-1-64961-552-7
                 eBook   978-1-64961-553-4

Library of Congress Control Number: 2021911514

DEDICATION

Dedicated in loving memory to Lorenzo "Logie" Meachum:
A friend, eternal scroll, and American National Treasure.
The Bruz.

ACKNOWLEDGMENTS

This is for my mom, Kathleen Collins (1946-2016),
God Bless your life. To my daughters, Daijara and Anyah.
Daddy's girls will always be daddy's girls. Love you.

CONTENTS

PROLOGUE

I n 1989, EMT workers wheeled Morehouse College student Joel Harris into the emergency room of Atlanta General Hospital, a few hours later he was pronounced dead, due to uncontrollable internal bleeding. After a brief investigation by school officials and local police, severe trauma to the abdomen, kidneys, hamstring muscles and buttocks consistent with prolonged physical abuse was determined as the cause of Harris's death. Immediately, Atlanta PD arrested members of Alpha Phi Alpha fraternity claiming that Joel Harris's death was the direct result of physical punishment he received during repeated beating sessions that Harris voluntarily took part in trying to become a member of Alpha Phi Alpha. The beatings and other forms of physical abuse Harris underwent were a part of a time-honored college tradition called pledging. "Pledging" is a term for the former initiation process into most college fraternities and sororities. Since Harris's death, pledging has been officially outlawed by all Black Greek fraternities and sororities, and most college campuses nationwide have explicit restrictions against the use of physical or mental challenge as a rite of passage into any campus organization. On the local level, however, college students haven't missed a beat since the Harris incident, and have in fact went the complete opposite direction, creating an underground sub-culture designed to circumvent the "official rules." Post-1989 pledging became more secretive and violent, but yet and still, persists. Why? My theory is that pledging persists because, despite the dangers involved, both members and non-members want pledging to survive. Moreover, the rise of "underground pledging" points to a desire for "danger" among Black Greeks and their would-be members.

On the national level, all Black Greek Organizations (BGO) were changed by the incident at Morehouse. On the local level, "altered" is a better descriptor. After, Harris's death BGO chapters across the country were hit with massive lawsuits from the parents and families of men and women killed or seriously injured during pledging processes. Ironically, when frats or sororities were sued, it was usually NOT the individual assailants who beat up or killed the pledge that bore the brunt of the financial weight for the assault or killing, it was the corporation that runs the brand name of the BGO that got sued. The individual members involved in the hazing incident, depending on the severity of the injuries to the pledge, received any punishment from expulsion to prison time. In an effort to save themselves as international business entities, the corporate managers of each respective BGO were forced to "water down" their respective intake processes, with the feeble hope that a tamer process would create a tamer Black Greek culture. "The Process," as it has become known inside Black Greek circles, was officially modified from an intense physical and psychological challenge to a "ceremony" in an effort to appease the white insurance companies that "oversee" the corporate managers of the BGO's.

By eliminating any mention of violence in the formal rites of initiation into BGO's, corporate brand mangers attempted to effectively change the public image and perception of what these organizations were about. This shift created a division within Black Greekdom that transformed BGO's on the national level into member managers, and on the local level, into underground fight clubs. The administrative image of Black Greek Organizations is well documented, but very little (if any) is written about Black Greek life from the grassroots perspective. I think that overlooking the wealth of folk wisdom hidden within this African American subculture might be more than just a loss to Black Greek Organizations. These organizations, and their members, impact American life well outside the confines of African- America.

Current studies regarding Black Fraternalism written by Walter Kimbrough, Ricky Jones, Matthew Huey, and Gregory Parks, though very useful, are steeped in academic language and an administrative epistemology. Although well researched, much (if not most) academic discourse on Black Greek fraternities focuses on the negative aspects of Greek life, almost always leaving little room for the perspective validity of the subjects being observed (namely, the fraternity members themselves). Studies like Black Greek 101 by Dr. Walter Kimbrough, for instance, down-right criminalize Black fraters. In essence, the developing body of scholarship surrounding Black Greek Fraternities is creating a situation that makes it look as if university and fraternity administrative power- players are turning undergraduate and non-conformist graduate BGO members of into a subaltern class.

This situation is problematic for many reasons, not the least of which is that much of the rich culture of Black Greek life has been lost in the chauvinism of the administrative perspective. The administrative perspective of Black Greek life elevates the survival of the organization (fraternity, sorority, college, or university) over the survival of the individual (student, fraternity or sorority member). The result is that college educated African Americans are being criminalized by the dozens. What's more is that, in recent years, members and aspirants have begun to accept this criminality as a part of the lure of Black fraternal life. Conversely, some other members and potential aspirants shy away from BGO's for this very same reason.

Black Greek life is a noble aspect of the African- American folk tradition, despite popular rhetoric that might suggest otherwise. The violence associated with Black Fraternal pledging is abhorrent to untrained eyes but approaching research on the subject with the aim at stopping it, without contextualizing the phenomena, has had the tendency of skewing the data uncovered, and overlooking many of the cultural contours inside the tradition that make the violence make sense. Ironically enough, understanding that violence "makes sense" inside Black fraternities is what has been missing from Black Fraternity scholarship. Understanding that violence makes sense inside these organizations, and moreover how it makes sense within these organizations, is crucial to understanding why every year young men (and to a lesser degree, women) line up waiting for their turn to get pummeled during "underground" pledge sessions. Once that question is answered, the process of altering the self- destructive tide of the Black fraternities can begin.

This novella is part fiction, part ethnography. This short work is a synthesis of years of learned and lived observation inside a Black Greek Organization. This is a novel about fraternities, but it reads more like a series of inter-connected short stories about people just being people. The common theme among all these stories is pledging "The Bruz" at Limestone College (Lambda

Gamma Chapter). No story in here is true to fact, but they are all true to life. My hope is that this work will be a contribution to the discourse that has already been laid bare on the issue of hazing. For privacy and legal reasons, names, places, and events have been altered to ensure that no one is incriminated in the tale that follows. The terms "Bruz," "Bruh," "Frat" and the like have been substituted for any specific reference to any particular person or organization. This is not only done for anonymity's sake, but it also done to make the experiences narrated in this book more universal to those reading it. Although I belong to a specific Black Greek Organization, the stories narrated here are an amalgamation of stories told to me by men of every type of fraternal background. They are designed to provide insight into all BGO's. It is my hope that rather than continuing the violence associated with our hallowed tradition that we learn from our mistakes and move forward toward a higher-level of reasoning about the best way to "educate" one another about fraternal living.

A. Chance, PhD.

THE OLD HEADS

A wise person once told me that, "Friendship is essential to the soul," and it was for this reason that I agreed to meet my old friend Dirty Red at the plot, rather than spend my lunch break smoking a blunt on the roof of the library, like I normally do. I was curious as to why Dirty Red wanted me to meet him at the plot rather than come to my office like everyone else normally does, but I figured it was Dirty Red, so anything was to be expected. I knew he didn't trust phones, camera's, police, or new faces, so his rationale for meeting at the plot was more than likely some sort of cleverly devised method of making things "look normal." I remember Dirty Red once telling me that the FBI bought Nextel so that they could keep taps on people's chirp conversations. I enjoyed talking to Dirty Red because he always talked in prison mumbles, coding every idea he uttered, constantly looking around, surveying the scene, and ensuring that no one was watching what he was talking about. I am far from a criminal, but whenever Dirty Red was around, I always feel like I should be, or at least have to try to be. In the twelve years we've been acquainted, I can honestly say I have yet to meet a Bruh who is as mobbed out with the frat as Dirty Red. In his words, "Lambda Gamma is La Costra Nostra, and we run our shit tight from the inside." In 2010, it had been Dirty's type of fanaticism that ruled the mindset of the Bruz at Limestone College. The group mentality has its flaws as well as its virtues.

Calvin "Dirty Red" Thomas has a motto: "I ONLY KNOW ONE WAY." This phrase means that pledging is the only way to become a real Bruh. This is how he feels, and this is how he lives. Dirty Red's whole day is spent maintaining an existence centered around the next time he gets to haze some undergraduate aspirants to the frat. He's forty years old, old school, and unashamed about how he lives his life. "I only know one way," were the first words out of his mouth as he walked toward me after stepping out of his cream-colored Cadillac Escalade. I smiled at him from behind my sunglasses because the 26-inch gold rims his truck sat on rose to their complete height once he exited the vehicle.

"You sittin' a little bigger than you used to be," I yelled back to him.

"Yeah, I just got 'em last pay day." He pointed back to his tires. He didn't get what I was saying.

I let him off the hook. "They look nice." His gold tooth was gleaming in recognition of my admiration of his biggest accomplishment in life. Gold rims from Rent- n-Roll. The truck wasn't his (yet) but it might as well be. Greg "Tiny" Whinette lent the truck to Dirty Red for the duration of his stay in Salisbury, with the instructions "make sure shits right."

Tiny Whinette, is a used car salesman by day, and a 1990 Lambda Gamma Bruh by night. Dirty Red is an '88 Bruh and was Tiny's Dean the first year he pledged Lambda Gamma but didn't make it. (Whinette pledged twice.) Now he is Tiny's right-hand man. Tiny is currently the vice-president of Pi Zeta, the graduate chapter in Salisbury. At the time he pulled Dirty

Red to the side, to give him his underground orders about managing the process, he was only Chapter secretary. This was three months ago, right before October elections. Since then, Dirty Red has been chosen to be the "Graduate Liaison to Limestone College." I wasn't at the meeting when Dirty Red got elected, but I think that Red was chosen because of all the Bruz in Pi Zeta Chapter, Dirty Red best represented the "Old Head" Lambda Gamma Bruz interests in undergraduate affairs. Lambda Gamma's attitude toward hazing can best be described as: "Haze the shit out of them young niggas because they want it and need it."

The executive body of the Old Heads felt it necessary to give themselves an "ace in the hole" so they gave Tiny a message to relay through their hand-picked nominee, Red. The Old Heads are a loose-knit conglomerate of Bruz who graduated from Limestone College in Salisbury, NC during any number of years from 1956 until now. Their official purpose is "to promote the interests of the fraternity on Limestone College's campus," but everyone knows that this is just a ruse to cover up their real purpose. The Old Heads want to create a voting bloc in the grad chapter that will ensure that the graduate and undergraduate chapters in Rowan County remain on the same page in reference to pledging. Of course, Black fraternity chapters are transitory in nature, and almost require that men come and go from the day-to-day operations of Bruh life on the local level. But there has always been, in Salisbury at least, a small contingent of Bruz, who after they graduated from Limestone, remained in Salisbury, or at least close enough to remain actively involved in the shared life of the fraternity chapters there. It is these Bruz, and Bruz like them, that keep pledging alive at Limestone College, and reinforce the continuity of a "tradition" that would surely be lost if it were left up to any other means to support it. This league of extraordinary gentlemen, threaten every year to topple the hegemony of National legislation within the frat simply by maintaining the internal order that keeps the frat afloat.

Red was chosen by Tiny for three reasons: 1) Being a recently released ex-felon, Dirty Red had a dynamic of free time within his daily schedule that was impossible for the other middle-aged Bruz to even try to lay claim to. 2) Very few Bruz have the level of fanatical dedication to the fraternity (in particular Lambda Gamma Chapter) that Dirty Red has and, 3) Even at age 39, Dirty Red had no problem enforcing his will with muscle and a pistol if need be. To be totally honest, even if the situation didn't call for muscle, Dirty Red might wreck a Bruh, just to do it, depending upon how he felt that day.

Tiny pulled Dirty Red to the side after the last graduate chapter meeting to give him instructions on how to manipulate the intake process. "Look here Red, Prophyte to Prophyte, these new niggas got to pledge. We have never taken over a paper line, and we ain't gonna start now. But things are changing over at the school, so we can't be as open wit' shit as we used to be. The school is getting that white money now, so you know they gonna wanna act all official about shit these days. We still gotta keep tradition alive though, but them dudes on the yard got to be on board. I don't care how long it takes, or how you do it, just make sure shits right. I got money riding on this school year."

"Don't worry 'bout shit Tiny, I got Fierce in my back pocket and you know them young niggas listen to him like crazy. I'll shoot him the word, and everything will be copasetic." Dirty Red smiled. His gold tooth shined every time he smiled, on the rare occasions that he did smile. Today he could not help but be elated. He was impressed with himself because a friendship he had maintained played an important part in the successful future of the frat. To him, that was everything. He was the Atlas of the frat, the weight of the world was on his shoulders, and he liked it.

The alumni Bruz at Lambda Gamma chapter have all, in recent years, gained an economic interest in Limestone College through membership in the graduate chapter of the Bruz. The non-profit alumni association "the Friends Foundation" that Pi Zeta formed in 2000, made up of members of the graduate and undergraduate members of the Bruz in Salisbury, raises money for Limestone College which, in turn, gives certain Bruz an influential voice in local politics, on and off campus. Bruz like Tiny were reaping the benefits of being an "upstanding community activist" as a side-effect of the community service that the frat was involved in. The Bruz, as a collective, use their influential voice to make sure that they never get charged for hazing their potential initiates. Individual Bruz, like Tiny, use their influence to augment their personal businesses.

The car matched Dirty Red's cream gators and sharply pressed Mississippi river boat gambler suit of the same color perfectly. The sun beamed off of his iceberg angled hair cut until he put on his French vanilla Kangol, and strolled casually up to the plot. Although it had been about twelve years since the first time I saw him, I could tell that the menace of time hadn't softened Dirty's disposition one bit. Dirty Red was still a stocky, less than six feet, big man. What nature didn't give him in vertical attributes he overcompensated with on his own in horizontal thickness. In the suit he had on, I couldn't tell if it was still all muscle underneath all that fabric, but when I first met him, anything that didn't ripple on his body bended.

By my estimation twelve years couldn't have put anymore than grown-man-will-knock-you-out weight on him. And if you let Dirty Red tell it, "Grown man and grandma shit" was all he was made of.

Our first encounter was homecoming 1998. He had just been released from prison after serving five years of a seventeen year sentence in Kentucky. This was my second Lambda Gamma homecoming, but he and I had never met because he was still locked up when we were on line. I met him right after that year's homecoming step show. It was a chilly October night, and the Bruz had just lost to the Sigma's. Our step team got disqualified for partial nudity on stage. My LB, Geno's pants fell down as he was performing. The crowd was shocked, but he just kept performing like it was all just a part of the show. I was on the hop team but wasn't mad because in my mind we set it out – the winning was in the doing it for the love of the fraternity. Plus, I was on the host committee for the Bruz, so I really didn't have time to sulk about anything anyways. My mission after the show was to run up to the plot, greet all my fans, grab a beer, and then drive to the hospitality room to finish setting up for the after party. No sooner than when I got ready to walk up onto the plot does Dirty Red stop me just short of rocks bordering it, to ask, "Who is you Nigga?" Normally I'd take offense to such an interruption of my flow, but I knew who Dirty Red was even before I'd met him. I'd heard the war stories. He was Lambda Gamma 1988, he pledged for three years straight because of bad grades. He was once thrown out of a second-story plate glass window in the boy's dormitory when he was online. He was the worst hazer in recent frat memory. And, he illegally read the '93 line into the frat, over the phone, from his half-way house!

After two years in the frat, I'd seen just about every type of whack job African-American manhood had to offer. Out Bruz, Crazy Bruz, Drunk Bruz, Nerd Bruz, and just down-right Mean Bruz; but none of them topped Dirty Red. What all of them had in common, like Dirty Red, was that they all were frat fanatics that lived out the entirety of their manhood under the guise of their Bruh identity. Dirty Red was that rare breed of 24/7 Bruz that, if you were from his chapter "damn it, you'd better be the Bruz 24/7 too" – "At least during your undergrad years, and especially, during your neo-year, damn it!"

At the heart of most Bruz like Dirty Red is a need for order, and community. Their violent xenophobia toward "outsiders" stems from a desire to be able to "control" life. Who is "real" and who is "fake" in this sense becomes a method of sorting out who belongs in your life and who doesn't. I replied, "3-Lambda Gamma- Spring 96, pleasure to meet you" and extended my hand to shake his when I met him. But Dirty Red just returned my grin with a mean mug. He hadn't seen me online, so in his mind, I must be lying to him about something. But he couldn't let me know that he knew I was lying.

"I know who you are Nigga. But do you know who I am? Better yet, can you tell me what we got in common?" He said. I was so fascinated by his raspy southern drawl that I couldn't quite comprehend what he was asking me. Before I could muster up a response, he shouted loud enough so that the hundred or so people within ear shot of us could hear, "We both Tre Dawgs Nigga!!!

Let's wreck!!!" Then he crouched down, ready to attack. A few people close to us moved out of the way so that they didn't get their homecoming bests soiled in the melee that was sure to follow.

7

For those feeling a little bit lost right now, "wrecking" is best described as wrestling, but if you ever seen a "wreck session" in real life you would more than likely classify it as a street brawl without any punches thrown (most of the time). According to Dirty Red, since he and I were both members of Lambda Gamma chapter and have the same line number, 3, "tradition" demands that we wrestle one another to "test" each other's manhood. My first thought was that "this big-ass jail nigga wants to get some empty aggression off on me," my second was that "wrestling with another man for no good reason sounds gay as hell."

"Naw Dirty Red, I think I'm just gonna go grab a beer instead? Would you like one?" was my response to him. I learned early on in the frat that Bruz talk shit to each other as a rhetorical game. If you side-step it, most of the time, you won't get caught up in the uglier side of Black fraternalism. Within the matrix of Black manhood, ignoring a man's aggression as if it isn't worthy of a retort is a cerebral way of crushing the spirit that made the man challenge you in the first place. Red knew this.

"Fuck you Nigga!!!" was his reply. I didn't have the energy to argue with him. I was tired from the show. Plus, I knew Dirty Red wasn't really being hostile (for Dirty Red). He was trying to see if I belonged or not. Was I worthy of the limelight I received as a Bruh at Limestone College. Our little exchange was my way of saying that it wasn't up to him to decide my worthiness. After I walked past him, I crossed over the plot, grabbed two beers out of the cooler, walked around the plot, being careful not to let any part of my foot touch any part of it while I had alcohol in my hand, and handed Dirty Red one of the beers, being thoughtful enough to open it for him. Dirty Red cussed me out every time he saw me after that during that homecoming. But I noticed he didn't say squat to any of the other young Bruz that were on the yard that year. We've been friends ever since.

The chapter is really tight-lipped about the circumstances that led to Dirty Red's incarceration, but the scuttle-bug around the yard is that it either had something to do with trafficking, racketeering, or murder. Whatever the case, all I know is that Dirty Red is a Don at Lambda Gamma now, and I've never had the heart or mind to ask him about it directly. My personal guess is that his incarceration was for murder, because Money, the deuce off of the '02 Pi Zeta line, told me that he was in school with Red at the time he went to jail for the first time, and he was pretty sure that "Dirty Red had a body on him." In fact, I remember when I was pledging Money, he was so scared of Dirty Red showing up to set that he paid his LB Vaughn to fake a heart attack while doing push-ups to avoid having to meet Dirty while he was online.

Dirty Red came to the plot to talk to me about homecoming. Over the years, he had come to view me as the point of contact for all things Bruh-related on campus. "Fierce, I'm gonna say it to yah straight, nigga. Every year it's like clockwork, the Bruz dominate Homecoming by out hosting all of the other organizations on campus. LG's job in the student structure of the school is to keep the Alumni happy and entertained long enough for the school to pick their pockets dry. This year the administration has offered to partner up with the Bruz on a fundraising party and shits got to be right. You on the yard, and is closest to them young niggas, so I'mma talk to you before I cuss 'em out. I want them neo's, old heads on the yard, and wanna-be's trying to get down in the spring, poppin' around this plot Friday and Saturday. Tiny got a tent and a barrel grill from his dealership that he's setting up Friday afternoon. The Bruz is gonna be grilling out on campus all weekend. The school is even sponsoring some of the food. We need you to have them boys find us a DJ to play music, to keep everybody entertained, and one or two of them are definitely gonna be doing the cooking. You know everybody gathers around our plot after the football game. And when we set our shit out right, they all follow us to wherever we are going all weekend. And the place we going this year is the Alumni Hospitality Ball, hosted by the Bruz."

"What does all of this have to do with me?" I asked. I was kind of peeved that he'd interrupted my mid- morning constitutional for this mundane shit.

"The graduate and undergraduate chapters get a cut of the proceeds, and the good word from administration come pledge season. Your job is to make sure all these dudes on the yard do their job. If shit fucks up, I'm holding you personally responsible."

"Call me guilty then, Dirty, because I'm not getting involved. I told y'all last year, I'm done."

THE DEAN OF EDUCATION

My name is Aiden "Fierce" Chance. I've been in the frat for almost 15 years, and have remained an active participant in the organization both inside and outside of official meetings since I came in. I have pledged over a hundred men, and never once killed anyone, or maimed any of them in any permanent way (except for maybe branding). I am a hazer. I haze. And I will continue to support doing so until the Bruz collectively come up with a better plan for making boys. What's more, I hope pledging comes back above ground so that the Bruz don't have to keep managing the process underground. But I refuse to keep risking life and limb to uphold a tradition that cannot sustain itself in the world that is to become. I know pledging is wrong now, and have curtailed my behavior, but many of my brothers, younger and older, continue to hold on to misguided notions of a tradition that is essentially destructive rather than constructive, as it purports to be. When I first got into the frat I thought that Nationals was just a bunch of complacent suits hell- bent on hampering the real-life vitality of the frat, but now I see, despite the divisions caused by Nationals' decision to stop supporting violence during initiation processes, that the non-violent intake process was a necessary innovation that had to come to pass if the frat was to grow as a unified body of educated men.

I came into the frat in 1996. That was a time I like to characterize as the "civil war era" of the Bruz. The big controversy back then was: "Who's real, and who's fake." Five years before then, National headquarters split the fraternity in two by publicly denouncing pledging and hazing, hand-in-hand. What was at stake for the Bruz was a complete loss of "control" over the intake process by local chapters. When the national body of the frat instituted "membership intake" as the new method of inducting members, it did so with no real clue as to how far reaching this seemingly small decision was. In essence, Nationals was breaking up families; or rather, they were introducing new members into families without the consultation of the local family members. New members were being introduced into tightly knit chapters, without a clue as to the history, background, character, or dynamics of the familial organizations to which they now belonged. In essence, the national body of the fraternity forgot that it was constituted by smaller local bodies. Can you image the attitude of your parents if they were forced to feed five new kids that they didn't know every year? These smaller bodies responded to the slight by rebelling. States' rights verses national law is the best way to characterize the situation. Local chapters by the dozens were refusing to comply with national by-laws, openly at times. The Fraternity responded to member defiance by asserting corporate control over the fraternity's brand name, and criminally prosecuting its own membership in some cases, in an attempt to maintain order. This didn't stop pledging though, but it clearly drew a line in the sand from which this war of attrition was to be battled.

Fraternity Chapters are small mafias inside a larger syndicate of mafias. In these families, Pledging has always been viewed as the best way to differentiate between who is really down for the cause and who is just along for the ride. "The cause," in this sense, is the longevity of the chapter and fraternity through the active involvement of each member. "Involvement" can mean anything from service in the graduate chapter to calling your line brothers and friends in the fraternity just to say "hello." In fact, life-long involvement in the frat is all of these activities and more. At times, active involvement in the frat can be too all-consuming, but in general every Bruh knows (or at least learns that) the frat is something you've got to carry, but you can't let it carry you. In the past, loyalty to the cause was enforced through parochial punishment. Now, membership selection leaves fraternal loyalty completely up to the voluntary actions of the aspirant. Bruz accept this decision as "the current mode of the day" on the surface of things. But deep down in their heart of hearts, many members don't trust initiates who didn't pledge, no matter what legal circumstances caused their lack of a good ass whipping.

When my fraternity split, chapters tore themselves apart trying to create a process of pledging that skirted around the austere legislative language of the new "intake processes" being instituted by all fraternities and sororities. A few chapters conformed, but most took to "hiding their boys" and not letting anyone who wasn't "close to the chapter" see their prospective initiates. The theory was that the fewer people who participated in a chapter's pledge process, the less likely chapters were to get caught or injure an initiate. But every line had to pledge, and had to be pledged by Bruz that the Bruz knew. This plan caused three internal problems that led to the civil war amongst the

Bruz I talked about earlier; 1) chapters became insulated, and began conforming to local conventions, over national mandates, "pledging" as well as "in-taking" in most cases; 2) new initiates pledged under this system came into the organization with a bifurcated prospective of fraternity politics that juxtaposed "nationals" and "the street Bruz," which fueled further division within the fraternity and further loss of national tradition; and, 3) on the undergraduate level, inter-chapter communication became strained or non-existent, fueling inter-chapter conflicts at mixed chapter events that began to look a lot like gang warfare. Added to all this was a large influx of working-class, African-American men into the American college system, many of whom were first-generation, who brought with them into the fraternity a personal values system shaped by the modern U.S. ghetto.

The frat, on the National level, started to resemble a fortune 500 company. But the frat, on a grassroots level, inevitably conformed to a street mentality when it came to who is real or not. As a result, for post-1991 Bruz, wreck or don't wreck became the mode of survival. All- in-all, the Bruz weren't trying to hurt one another or themselves, but the violence of the 90's caused many older Bruz to shy away from their personal commitment to the frat because the rules of engagement that sustain the Bruz were only sustainable within the confines of the frat. More than one Bruh had been embarrassed in front of his girlfriend or wife by an over-zealous young Bruh challenging them to wreck out in public. I remember hearing about two Bruz wrecking at Concord Mills, on some old "who's real, who's not," and one of their wives going into labor after being knocked over during the brawl. An unfortunate incident that was never reported, but nonetheless indicative of the downward slope we were all sliding down.

The 90's was almost like a witch hunt amongst the Bruz. At every Bruh function, at every Bruh event, within the matrix of every Bruh interaction, there was always the confrontation about "who's been to the fight club, and who hasn't?" Bruz became so transfixed on who pledged and who didn't that most of us lost sight of the traditions we were trying to uphold in the first place. Black fraternities are supposed to be about manhood, friendship, academic achievement, community involvement, and mutual support. So you tell me, where does two grown-ass men tussling in a parking lot fit into all of that? Lord knows that none of the founders envisioned that their future frat brothers would reduce their allegiance to the organization to a fist fight in the park, but that's exactly what used to happen at damn near every undergrad (and even some Grad) Bruz event in the 90's. My explanation for it is that some Black Men tend to unnecessarily elevate certain secular allegiances to the level of the sacred. In this case, the sacred space becomes the entire frat for the individual member, and they take it upon themselves to purge the fraternal sacred of all its impure interlopers via a good wreck session. I've seen it get so heated in a room full of Bruz that the weakest one in the room wound up in the cut, getting paddled, repenting for not remembering his oath to stay involved in the life of the organization.

Don't get me wrong though, the Bruz aren't criminals or thugs (most of us). We really do love each other (in our own way). We get up and go to work every day. Take care of our families. Do community service. And try our best to exemplify the role of a "Positive Black Man" to the fullest. But, as a measure of self-management, not self-mutilation, we go hard at keeping our circle tight. The violence in the frat is tolerated to the level that it exists because, in function, the violence is a self-regulating process. Everybody stays in line because nobody wants it to happen to them.

My line was "fortunate" enough to have the experience, but even this didn't shield us from being baptized by fire into the civil war after we went over. Our first few road trips to other schools to meet our national frat brothers were literally visits to rival gang turfs. (Or at least it felt that way.) Every neophyte in the fraternity was given the prime directive by the Old Heads of their respective chapter, "protect the yard." Ostensibly, the yard was being protected from "fake Bruz" sneaking onto your yard, sullying up the Bruz image. No sooner than we stepped on to another chapter's yard, we were confronted by 10-20 Bruz wanting to know who we were, where we "pledged at," and what we're doing at "their" school. If any question wasn't answered to satisfaction, it was a wreck session right then and there until someone got tired or seriously mad. When it was all over, the Bruz would grip up (shake hands), teach each other something, and the host chapter would get to hosting. A set out usually consisted of free fried chicken and beer to the visitors, and the inside track on some female attention. My line never had to do too much wrecking we didn't want to do, but I've seen plenty of Bruz have one of those nights where the sound of their back hitting the ground well in advance of their feet is all anyone at the plot could remember for the rest of the party.

Although pledging had recently been outlawed by the school and the frat, our line pledged underground as a matter of choice, rather than force, to eliminate all doubt there may have been that Limestone College Bruz still pledged. We all agreed, "none of us want to be paper." "Going paper" was our way of describing the then new "intake" process of membership selection that required aspirants to forego the pledge process all together, memorize a "history packet," take a test, and then venture out into the world of the Bruz without any further guidance. We all knew that nothing in Black world was ever that easy. It felt like a set-up by the national headquarters: "Pay your money, recite these words, and then go play nicely with all the other boys wearing these fancy shirts we're going to make you pay for." Our situation was made worse by the fact that we didn't have any immediate "Old Heads" on the yard to tell us how to run the chapter, or even how to be members at the national level. By 1996 most of the '92 Bruz had graduated and left Salisbury. A couple of the renegade '93 Bruz still lived in the area, but they weren't in school, or allowed to participate in any public fraternity events. Of course, they hung out with the Bruz, but there were very well-known rifts even amongst them and the '92 Bruz who took them over. So, needless to say, there was little in the way of a leadership support system, on the local level for the Bruz. Limestone hadn't had a line of Bruz for four years before we crossed. The '92 line was kicked off the yard for trying to pledge the would-be '93 line, in the fall of 1992. The 1993 line became the first, and only, "renegade" line in the chapter. For those unfamiliar with the term, "Renegade Bruz" are fraternity members who have been read into the fraternity without national consent. The phenomenon was very rare up until the 90's, but the practice surged during the initial era of intake. "Renegading" Bruz has calmed down since the millennium, but every now and then, you'll still find a

Bruh who has a story about why his process wasn't "quite right."

Back then, the school's method for handling hazing violations was to suspend the chapter long enough for the current members to graduate, usually 3 years, and then reactivate the chapter with a new group of initiates who have no connections to older members of the chapter. The hope was that a lack of continuity in chapter membership would eventually lead to conformity to school and national rules concerning hazing. In Limestone College's case, this was mistake number one of many. The Lambda Gamma and Pi Zeta chapters have a shared history that supersedes the confines of a business arrangement. These men live with one another. Of course, they are going to do everything in their power to maintain the power structure in their favor, because it suits their needs. Faith worked with ingenuity.

The ace of the '92 line, Anthony "Slow Jams" James, used his campus fame as a college basketball star to get a job in the financial aid office after he graduated. He was never suspended for hazing because no one ever implicated him specifically in the case that got the rest of his LB's suspended. Slow Jams never really saw the '93 line because they were pledging during basketball season. 1993 was the year Limestone College almost won the CIAA tournament. Slow Jams was the star point guard. He led the league in assists and steals that year. He had 20, double doubles. When the school's student activities office contacted the national office of our fraternity to reactivate the chapter, the fraternity via the local grad chapter contacted Slow Jams to oversee the local initiation process. Being a college administrator put Slow Jams in a precarious situation, but the survival of chapter tradition was important enough to him to put his career and reputation on the line to teach us the "old school" way. After much convincing of him by us of our sincerity, he pledged my line, "the 10 Disciples of Faith," underground.

During our process, Slow Jams taught us national and chapter history, and introduced us to other members of our chapter during "special" pledging sessions. We learned the basics of how to step and felt the threshold of our own personal tolerance for pain. Our "Hell Night" introduced us to representatives from every chapter in our region. Slow Jams went against conventional wisdom and let us have a Hell Night open to other chapters so there would be no question that we were "real." As I said earlier, by 1996, LG had been off the yard for four years. No Bruh who wasn't immediately a part of our underground process could verify whether or not we pledged. Slow Jams' name carried a little weight, but word on the streets (and even the yard) was that our line was going to be paper. That year, every other organization on the yard that was allowed to hold a membership intake process "forced" their local undergraduate chapter to go paper.

Slow Jams called Bruz from every chapter in our region asking them to see "his boys" on their Hell Night, because he didn't want anyone ever bringing that "real or fake" argument to Salisbury. Lord have mercy, why did he do that? The Bruz responded to his call with vigor. I hear that a few of the Bruz who attended nicknamed our Hell Night "the Super Bowl" because so many different chapters were involved. Two more lines were supposed to be there with us, but their old heads stopped them from coming because the risks outweighed the reward. To give you a clearer picture of how many Bruz a contingent like the Super Bowl involves, consider this.

Our region covers both North and South Carolina. Within those two states alone, there are well over 50 chapters. Averaging two Bruz per chapter (and no one rolled with only two Bruz from their chapter), that would be about one hundred seemingly angry black men in your face "pretending" that they are going to kill you-some even going so far as trying to kill you. I'm not sure if everyone there got a chance to personally beat us, but there was enough beating going on that night to estimate that each man in attendance got five licks off of me and my nine LB's.

I can still remember marching single file with all my line brothers into the abandoned football field our Hell Night took place in. We all had on matching jeans, white t-shirts, and black boots. We looked tough. We were all scared shitless though. We were locked up chest-to-back so that if any of the Bruz tried to snatch us out of line, we could grab hold of the man in front of us to secure our spot. For intimidation purposes we were allowed to "march into our doom." From the gates entrance I could see the entire field, which was a fearsome canvass of Bruz of all shapes and sizes. Some stepping, some wrecking, some laughing, and some drinking; but the large majority of them were transfixed on tonight's victims (us). Before we descended to the bottom of the hill where the field was at, about ten Bruz formed an impromptu gauntlet for us to walk through. Within the gauntlet were fists, feet, elbows, and paddles. I tried to protect my LB in front of me, but I only received blows for my diligence. My LB behind me tried to protect me, but there was a Bruh on each one of his arms straining in earnest to force him to break his hold on me so they could take him off to the side by himself. At one point, I tried to lift my head up to see where we were walking to, but I only received a punch to my right cheek for the effort. From that point on, I kept my head down as much as possible, gaining my bearings by the hash marks on the football field. Everything I experienced that night after crossing the threshold of that gauntlet was an out-of-body experience. I saw the worst abuses of the human body imaginable re- enacted on me and my line brothers. Calisthenics, torture, fighting, human beer pong, and mayhem. One Bruh was trying to light line my brother Fredo on fire until Slow Jams punched him in the mouth for not being able to justify why he was trying to burn a pledge. Our rule at LG is that any time you put hands on a man, it has to be to teach him something, and that that something has to be worth the punishment inflicted on him during the learning process. Slow Jams taught that Bruh that violators get violated. He also showed everyone in attendance that he did have some measure of control over what was going on, even if it didn't look that way.

Running around that field that night getting rocked was the freest I've ever been. Even though I was scared, and it hurt, I got a chance to unleash the sleeping giant within me. I fought fear fearlessly. I stood up for my LB's, I accepted blows I didn't have to willfully, I dished a few good ones on the low too. I was one of the wild boys. As rough and tumble as football scrum, pledging was my new rugby. I said to myself, "This is Real!" I still can remember a Bruh from Chi Beta chapter ramming his boney elbow into my chest while a Sigma Epsilon Bruh was teaching me to recite "Invictus" verbatim.

Understandably, most people outside the frat don't like hazing, and a growing number inside Black Greek Organizations don't like it either. They look at pledging, and the hazing that accompanies the ritual, as simple-minded savagery. ("A bunch of niggas beating each other up," is how one "expert" put it.) But pledging is much more than that. I don't really like beating people up myself, but having gone through it, and witnessing the fraternal life of those who enter Black Greek Organizations without having pledged, helps me to understand pledging (and the violence that is part-and- parcel of it) as one of the many necessary evils of life. Pledging is a reckoning period –cultural space that provides a physical (yet wholly symbolic) challenge that becomes an "accomplishment" that the aspirant can look back on as proof that they are as great as they think they are. (Even if that "greatness" only exists within the limited space of the Bruz.)

This may seem weird when observed outside the context of who the Bruz are, but when you consider that the Black men who make up the Bruz are sharing their pain with one another during the pledge process, and that the fraternity members and the aspirants are trying to create a pledging process that promotes self- and group- leadership, you'll see that pledging is a rite of passage that fits the dynamics of the environment it tries to symbolically represent. When you look at the total scheme of the scheme, it is clear that for many, pledging is a vital transformative period in their lives. It helps them cope with rigors of day-to-day civil living.

Most Black men in America, born prior to 1985, grew up in extreme poverty and ignorance. Even today, the large number of poor and working-class first- generation Black male college students are astounding. Many come to college from relatively violent environments a million miles removed from mainstream middle-class society. However, the intended result of matriculation into a western education is just that— turning them into a middle-class participant in American society. The gap in values (low income vs. middle income) must be bridged in some way to forge a path for African-American "success" amid an oppositional environment. In my opinion, pledging, and the day-to-day violence in the Frat, in its own dysfunctional way, helps bridge this gap. Pledging is cathartic. Once the catharsis is over, young Black fraters are better able to socialize in a world (the frat) that prepares them for integration into mainstream society. Despite their foils, the Bruz, individually and as a group, all aspire to the loftiest ideals of American society. Our problem is that we just go to too far an extreme to maintain order within that order.

The movie fight club is the best analogy I can use to describe the relationship between the pledger and the pledge in a Black Greek Organization. Bruz and pledges enter into an implied social contract with one another that allows each to see the darkest side of the other. Every year, across the country, adult men come together in clandestine union to test their individual mettle in group battle. Bruz on one side, pledges on the other. But unlike the movie fight club, these men aren't entering into the fight club to create public mayhem. On the contrary, they are participating in this fight club to symbolically challenge themselves to the rigors of African-American leadership. I know to outside eyes pledging seems to be an idiotic manifestation of ritualized barbarity. But within the confines of the Black Greek underground, the experience is everything. For a brief moment in their otherwise mundane and misguided lives, pledgee's are allowed space for their inhibitions to be loosened enough to surrender to the fear we all silently embrace—being alone, helpless, and meaningless. Pledges are forced to confront, and attempt to overcome, these psychological hindrances during their pledge process. As even the most amateur psychologist will tell you, fear is programmed into individuals by society from birth on. The Bruz seek to de-program their initiates of some of this fear, by introducing them to a rush of terror. The hope is that the initiates learn that they can overcome any adversity, no matter how trying their individual ordeal may be.

The fight club allows Pledgers an outlet to vent their natural manly rage as well. While placing them in the position of custodianship for another man's life; namely the pledge, it asks them to be their punishers as well. Being placed into the role of the enforcer of fear for the pledge is a huge responsibility. For nine to ten weeks (longer or shorter, depending on where you go) pledges are taught that fear is a part of life. Aspirants are also taught that fear is only a small part of life, and that this small part of life can be managed by basking in the safety of togetherness. The beatings and tribulations associated with hazing are symbolic of the bumps and bruises we absorb from day-to-day living. True, some people do go too far during their pledging, but most don't because they know that being in charge of pledging another person is a responsibility, and moreover, they know that they are only acting as if they are trying to hurt the aspirant. Bruz who let their personal rage get the best of them during a set should be severely checked before they do serious harm to an initiate (and usually are). The fear and anger inherent in the experience is only supposed to be symbolic.

It is not uncommon to hear a pledge, or Bruh that has been pledged, say that life is "hard, but fair." This phrase is a hind-sight reference to the lessons that they've learned while online, namely, the temporality of pain and fear. Believe it or not, this lesson helps, and is of valuable use for the average Black man. This message resonates on a highly personal note for many African-American men because our group history is marred with instances of physical brutality both at home and out in public. From childbirth onward we are taught that a good beating is the best way to "teach" a Black man a lesson. The culture of pledging (at least as I've experienced it and doled it out) harnesses the power of this method of corporeal instruction into something seemingly positive. I tell every group of pledge's I visit, "If you want to learn something, get in the cut, and let this wooden paddle teach you everything you need to know."

Throughout our lives, time and time again, we are shown that adversity is our best professor. Most of us who've been through a pledge process jokingly say, "if I don't mind, it don't matter" because after the shock of violence is over, you're no worse for wear, and you get to schmooze with other Black men trying to "make it" just like you. The implied lesson is that no turmoil is designed to last forever, and in fact, most of life's tortures are merely preparation for the better parts of living. Of course, not everyone who pledges, or gets pledged understands this implied lesson. Nor does every member of the fraternity automatically become your friend just because you pledged, but the experience links members (at least psychologically) into an elite circle of people who feel the way I do, and these people are involved in every different type of endeavor known to man. What Black man worth his balls wouldn't want to be a part of something like that?

THE CHAPTER

When I joined the frat I didn't think that I would become a lifetime hazer. As I said before, when I first got into the frat I abhorred hazing. I figured pledging a fraternity would just be one those things I did in college for kicks. My focus was always academics, so joining any organization was just something I was doing so I could put that I participated in college life on my resume. But the frat woke something up in me. I became something more, something I should be, a leader, someone I will become when I grow up. I took my pledge process seriously, personally, mystically even. As a rule of thumb, I didn't share the details of it with anyone, not even my line brothers who went through it with me. But I'm sharing the details of my experience with you now so that others who lead similar lives will have a guidepost by which to judge the normalcy of their actions.

When I got into the frat I told myself I wasn't just going to talk about how much I loved the frat, I was going to "live the frat." Even when my LB's wanted to trade war stories about who had it the hardest on line, I rarely joined in because I realized pledging wasn't the biggest or best part of the frat experience. Plus, the gravity of what had happened to us gave me mixed emotions about glorifying violence as our unifying experience. In my mind, we had voluntarily let some strangers whoop our ass, but it didn't prove or disprove anything about us. To my LB's it was no biggie, pledging was just how things are done, they couldn't wait to do it to someone else next year. To me, our pledge process was a sacred, yet traumatic, rite that shaped the texture of the rest of my frat experience. One of my biggest fears in life was getting jumped, and to me, that's what pledging felt like. The only difference was that this jumping was voluntary on my part, and I didn't fight back with blows. I'd survived it, proudly, without a visible mark on me. My heart was scarred though, and I wore my pledge process as a personal badge of honor. Far from wanting to do it to someone else, however, I wanted the violence of pledging to end after I first went over. It wasn't until I graduated that I actually started swinging wood on the Bruz. After witnessing the barbarism of underground pledging first-hand, I came to the conclusion that no other man needed to pledge after me to get into the frat. There had to be a better way to develop young Black men into leaders. The shock and trauma tactic of the Bruz, though modeled after the mold set forth for us by society, was too dangerous a practice to continue performing in modern America's hyper-litigious environment. To me, it made no sense to continue to risk jail time and a lawsuit just to beat some college kid's ass.

I carried this sentiment with me throughout my undergrad experience. I participated in the official intake process, and showed my neck at set a few nights, but everybody knew that I wasn't a hazing Bruh. We pledged two lines before I graduated, but I didn't touch one of them. I saw all of them pledge, of course, and I interacted with them vigorously; but I didn't harm anyone physically because I knew that that wasn't my role in the frat. My role was to be the voice of reason, a dean of education, rather than a dean of pledging.

By the late 90's, when I came in, pledging had moved so far underground that it was clearly on its way to becoming its own culture. This new culture threatened to destroy all of Black Greekdom, or at least turn it into to something other than the middle-class social clubs that frats and sororities were being publicized as being. On the surface of things all looked well in Greek world, but on the inside, the inmates were running the asylum. Things got so bad for a while that the Limestone College student activities department expected at least one organization out of the divine nine to catch a hazing charge each spring, and the Greeks didn't disappoint. The Bruz didn't catch a case until '93, which was ironic because the chapter prides itself on its rough and tumble image. LG has been straight ever since then though, in part, because of the innovations we brought into the fold with us. What my line did, when we came in, was have the financial aid director, who was a Tau Psi Bruh, get us assigned to work-study in Student Affairs, so that we could work our way into the upper echelon of campus life. As work-study students we were kept abreast of all campus gossip concerning fraternities and sororities. We took work- study in Student Affairs so that we would know if our names were buzzing, and what for, before the word reached the wrong hands. Fortunately, most of us were choir boys, outside of being notorious hazers, so we were usually more so aware of what was going on with all the other organizations than whether or not the Bruz were in trouble. What I found out from my eavesdropping was that everything that is going on within larger society is going on within Black Greek-Lettered Organizations. People are just average people, no matter what color shirt they might happen to be wearing.

Lambda Gamma is not your average chapter in the frat. Like most undergrad chapters, however, LG is holding on tightly to its pledging "tradition," even though it's been outlawed for almost twenty years now. Lambda Gamma's tradition of hazing has become down-right institutionalized, and I don't think even the Grand Frater in the sky could stop it now. My line was just a link in the chain; where that chain ends, no one knows. Only at LG do you have all facets of the membership intake process working in concert to bridge the gap between the national goals of the corporate office, and the day-to-day demands of local Black fraternal life. I remember when I first transferred to Limestone College my roommate, Big Herb (LG 92), told me, "This shit has been going down since March 27, 1927 (The Chapter's founding date) and it ain't gonna stop no time soon." He may have actually been right.

Limestone College's president, vice-president, student activities director, and chief of campus police are all Bruz. All of whom pledged pre-1990. Although well off into their respective careers, none of them have a vested interest in enforcing hazing legislation, just so long as no one gets hurt or so upset that they tell "outsiders" about what's going on. '92 got jammed up because, a few of them tried to pledge some guys who didn't have the grades, the mistake wasn't discovered until the five young men were about to go over, so the chapter was put in the position of telling these men that they endured a semester of torture for nothing. A few of the Bruz in the chapter were salty, and felt the stalled process was more bureaucratic nonsense, designed to micro-manage undergraduate affairs. In reality, the stalled intake process was due more so to chapter negligence, than a concerted effort by anyone to stop the process. At any rate, some of the Bruz were scared that the jilted pledges would tell what had happened to them to force the frat to take them in, so four LG members, with the help of Dirty Red, took it upon themselves to initiate the five members of 1993 line without national consent. These Bruz were recognized by most of Lambda Gamma as Bruz, but they weren't officially enrolled on the fraternity's national roster yet. The frat threatened to sue, and the initiates threatened to counter-sue. The dispute was finally settled by the fraternity begrudgingly capitulating to the demands of the situation and reading "the Five" in with our line in 1996. Most of them anyways, the #3 off of that line, Haywerd "Big Baby" Mills, graduated in 1994, and no one has heard from him since. To this day there is a heated dispute within the chapter as to whether or not 93 and 96 are one line, or two. Our line looks at itself as a separate thing from them.

LG is the 34th chapter started in the fraternity. It was originally founded at Rosenberg Liberal Arts College in Chicago in 1927, but the chapter transferred its charter to Limestone College in Salisbury, NC in 1946. Limestone is one of the few remaining "Black" Historically Black Colleges in the United States. The school prides itself on producing from its ranks some of the most notable African-Americans in American history. Two national presidents of Black Greek-Lettered Organizations came from Limestone. One of which, was an LG Bruh. Legend has it that the transfer was a forced move caused by the banning of LG on Rosenberg's campus due to the high frequency of excessive violence associated with the organization on campus. Officially, the Chapter went inactive at Rosenberg in 1941 due to low membership numbers as a result of World War II. At that time, Clayton Bartle, one of the last Bruz initiated at Rosenberg, took a job at Limestone as a P.E. instructor. A veteran himself, Bartle believed in the rules of regimental military discipline, and saw himself as a redeemer of sorts for every African-American male who came under his sway. In 1946, Bartle, and two other Bruz who worked at Limestone, Asa Hillard and Joseph Bramble, convinced the school's reluctant administration to re-charter the Lambda Gamma chapter at Limestone as a measure to promote student morale. Limestone was in desperate need of students during the 1950's so the President skeptically capitulated to student demands for Black Greek Organizations on campus despite the Christian objections of some very prominent alumni.

I was fortunate enough to hear Bramble, then 77 years old, speak at a chapter Founder's Day banquet in 1997, right before he died. I was way past tipsy, so I don't remember the complete details of the entire night, but I can still feel how moved I was by the power of Bramble's words. In his brief address, Bramble said, "back then, we didn't have any real Black heroes to look at, so it was up to us to become those hero's that were so desperately needed in the community. The frat was our way of taking the reigns of leadership. We weren't trying to be anything special, but we knew we weren't ordinary." He was right. Those men were anything but ordinary. According to Chapter legend the charter line at Limestone "the 13 Knights of Justice" we're pummeled by Hilliard (line name Lumber Jack), Bramble (line name Woody T. Haze), and Bartle (line name Justice).

After the banquet was over, I got a chance to spend a little more time with Brother Bramble at the hospitality suite we rented for his stay. He made me drink this really strong Scotch with him, as he reminisced. He called it "smooth" but to me, it burned just as much as any other alcohol, only in a different way. He told me that "one year, Brother Bartle lost his job as head groundskeeper, because the school's president heard how hard he was pledging the president's nephew, who was trying to go over that semester." According to Bramble, Bartle habitually saved a special place in hell for the President's nephew, Jason "Wheepy Time" Teaparty, because he thought he was soft. "What got Justice fired was the ass whoopin' he put on Wheepy after he found out Wheepy had been ditching his French class for two weeks to go see some girl he met in Charlotte. It took Brother Hilliard, who was vice-provost of annual giving (the youngest person in the history of the school to hold such a high-ranking title), two semesters of quiet begging to convince President Carter to grant Bartle clemency." Bramble chuckled, "Good thing they wasn't so much into prosecuting pledgers back then. Even the school looked at it as all fun and games." At his funeral, Brother Bramble had the initials of the fraternity stitched into the lining of his casket.

Bruz like Bramble, Hillard, and Bartle were pioneers. They may not have changed the world, but the chapter legacy that they have left behind has certainly changed the world for the thousand or so men who've crossed the burning sands at Limestone College. Today, Lambda Gamma is still alive and well, and we teach our new initiates the story of the chapter founders alongside the national organization's history with the goal of instilling in our pledges a sense of purpose by tying their personal linage to a noble tradition of Black Male excellence. The truest details of the founders' story have been lost in the annals of oral history, but the intended message remains the same. Bramble summed it up best in his address to the undergraduates by paraphrasing a famous quote from one of our national founders. He said, "The frat is not an activist organization, but it is an organization full of activists."

THE UNDERGRAD BRUZ

Being a member of a Black Greek-Lettered Organization is an experience like no other. But being an undergrad member of the Bruz at Limestone College is as close to superstardom as most African-American men experience in our mundane little lifetimes. Lambda Gamma makes a concerted effort to mold its Bruz for the limelight, encouraging them to take leadership positions in the fraternity, both locally and nationally. My theory on why Nationals is so adamant about controlling undergraduate affairs is that they realize the profit-earning potential of an organization that promotes a positive Black male image. They also realize that leaving control of the organizations to a bunch of inexperienced college kids is economic suicide. Undergrads rebel because they believe that they have, or should have, a choice in determining how they're image is used – at least, in terms of initiation. "The frat is all about that money nowadays," is what you'll hear being said around most plots. But in all fairness to the frat, even if this is true, the frat isn't doing anything but manipulating the variables to its own advantage. The superstructure of the organization has to survive, if the microstructure of it hopes to continue. I tell all the undergrads I come in contact with, "Enjoy your undergrad days, but don't get too caught up in the politics of the situation, because it will drive you crazy." Why should they waste their lives arguing when they could be out doing something important with their youth?

LG is a "stepping chapter," meaning we raise money for chapter events by winning step show championships across the country. So, when I say being a member of our chapter as an undergrad is like superstardom, I mean it. Last year we lost a national competition in Atlanta to a group of Kappa's who had a white boy. But we still placed high enough to bring home money to the chapter, and that's what really mattered to us. Our goal was to represent the Bruz, and win dough, so that we would have the loot necessary to pay for our annual Mardi Gras Ball in April. Mardi Gras is our chapter's signature event. The ball raises money for freshman scholarships and acts as an annual reunion of all our chapter's alumni members. It is also the event we use to formally introduce our newest members to the community. Mardi Gras weekend is our chapter's informal version of a national convention. Being a step group as well as frat brothers is a tough job, but our system works to produce better Black men.

Doing live performances, stepping, hosting parties, organizing community service events, and traveling to conferences are all valuable life experiences for young African-American men. Although, admittedly, most of the Bruz don't understand the full benefit of these leadership training experiences, inevitably, they produce Black leaders. The discipline it takes to fully participate in the Black Greek experience as an undergrad is a primary reason that the physical punishment side of our introductory training process -pledging- is so needed. Pledging is a counterbalance. The structure of that brief experience keeps the undergrads humble and self- regulating. If done right, a person's pledge process can help forge them into an effective leader. My quantitative proof for this assertion is the large number of American- Americans who "pledged undergrad" and are now in "leadership" positions. Those who know how to freak it right, parlay the undergrad experience into their own personal pattern of social success. (Look at Jesse Jackson) Of course, pledging isn't the only way to produce a leader, but it is a time-honored method for producing Black student leaders.

At an HBCU, when a person joins an organization, they enter into a new realm of public celebrity. Their singular person becomes the living embodiment of WHAT their organization stands for. Their every action is being judged by the standard of what an AKA is, or a Que is, or a Sigma, an Alpha, a Kappa, a Delta, etc. etc. The whole is greater than the sum of its individual parts. During a person's neophyte year, their every action is automatically equated to what a leader should or should not be. Unfortunately, most Black Greek-Lettered Organizations don't recognize this as their best opportunity to create a "teaching moment" so they brush the neophytes off as "immature" and "unworthy" of the "knowledge" the older ones have about the frat/the sorority/life. Most older members completely ignore the real-life dynamics of the average neophyte's life, shrugging off the validity of the neo's search for a role model within the immediate confines of his/her organization. As a result, the growing pains of a person becoming more socially aware of their surroundings are left unresolved. In reality, this period of socialization is the perfect opportunity to teach neo's how to be a leader of themselves, and a leader within the organization. The Bruz at Lambda Gamma recognize the neophyte year as a "teaching moment," at least they do now that I'm in charge of the process and use it (and the entire undergraduate experience) as an opportunity to develop a spirit of personal leadership in all our members.

It's no wonder Bruz like Dirty Red and Tiny want in on the undergrad action. But I keep them and all the other old heads at a relatively safe distance from the prospective initiates until just about time for them to go over because I've learned that it's best to not let Bruz and their personal agendas outweigh the overall safety of the pledges. It is important for a Dean to be vigilant of the older Bruz in their chapter during pledge season because there are any number ways the young Bruz can be misused to promote an individual Bruz personal agenda. Cars for instance – a line of ten men could either be the consumers who buy ten cars when they graduate from college; or ten salesmen who sell cars, after they graduate. In Tiny's mind I'm sure the next line that goes through will be both. I've noticed how he operates over the years, and I don't like it. He's very sneaky. He slithers around set whispering obscenities in the pledges ears as they try to recite their literature. He finds out who the softest one is and zero's in on that man while swinging wood. Everyone else gets a mercy tap from Tiny, except for his man of choice. When Tiny's victim for the night gets in the cut, Tiny brings out his personal rattlesnake "Lucretia." Lucretia is a three foot long, one-and-a-half inch thick oak paddle, Tiny had specially crafted, with a twelve inch handle, and a two foot flat smooth paddle surface on one side, with the frats initials engraved on the other side. When Lucretia gets to swinging, the person getting hit has no choice but to listen to the person that is doing the hitting. Tiny wants to ensure that there is going to be a "real" process this year because he uses the process to "catch" the new Bruz before they get in. His method of doing things makes the pledge who is getting broken down fear Tiny, and those whom he shows mercy feel as if they are at his mercy. Every year he tries to convince the Young Bruz that helping him do his personal business helps the chapter do its fraternal business. "Let's make the frat work for all of us," he says. Sure, a couple of undergrads have gotten jobs at his auto lot, and even more have gotten into cars because of him, but beyond the surface of things Tiny's agenda is limiting the new Bruz to his vision of the world which ultimately moves no further than living in Salisbury and driving a new car. Not on my watch!

THE ADVISOR

I work in the library at Limestone College, and I am the Chapter Advisor now, have been for most of the past five years. The last Brother to hold the position before me, officially, was impeached. In a very real sense, you can say that I do have my hands on everything Bruh related in Salisbury. But like I told Dirty Red, I am not involved in the underground business anymore. It's just too dangerous. The frat is really sending Brothers to jail over that shit, and quite frankly, I've got much, much better things to do with my time than sit in a cell reminiscing about my glory days as a Bruh. I took the Library job to help me pay my way through grad school, not to be involved in the frat. But five years later, a master's degree, and a slumping economy that isn't really hiring teachers like that, and I'm still here shelving books 8am-5pm Monday-Thursday, and Saturday 10am- 6pm. I am still faithfully involved in what transpires with the undergraduate chapter of the Bruz at Limestone College, but I don't participate in much of it that often. I originally said "no" to the idea of being the advisor because I thought it would take away from my studies. But, after years of ducking the responsibility, responsibility ultimately fell on the shoulders of the Bruh strong enough to carry it.

When Slow Jams left Limestone to work for Duke University, someone from the chapter had to fill the crucial void his absence created. Reluctantly, both chapters accepted Brother Theodore Little's self- nomination for advisor because, sadly, other than myself, no other Brother in the graduate chapter fit the necessary qualifications to be considered an advisor. According to the frat, a brother had to have been in the frat for at least five years, or a college administrator for an equal amount of years, to be an advisor. If Little wouldn't have spoken up during our meeting about the undergraduate advisors position, the graduate chapter would have probably nominated me for the position anyways, because I was the only young LG Bruh who still worked on campus. We tried having a non-LG Bruh act as the advisor, once, before Little or Slow Jams ever came into the picture, but according to Dirty Red, "after that the Bruz learned quick why once was one too many. Outsiders need to stay outside." Red covered his Tennessee mouth to whisper to me during the meeting when Little was nominated, "Just because we all in the same frat doesn't mean we all in the same business." He never elaborated on the thought after that, but I got the drift.

I didn't really have a personal problem with Little. To me, he was just another loyal member of the organization trying to do what he thought was right. Plus, the Bruz needed to civilize themselves anyways. Adding a reverend to the mix couldn't make things that much worse. In the mind of the Grad chapter, Little's presence was supposed to calm down the violent turn undergrad hazing was taking on campus. The undergrads were for any plan that would keep them from going to jail. In 2001, all the Greek organizations on Limestone College's yard were still hazing to some degree. The problem was that they were doing it very badly. Some group was always getting kicked off the yard or investigated. And it was always for the same thing: hazing. In 1999, one guy went to the hospital with a broken ear drum he received after being slapped too hard while pledging. That same year, a whole chapter of Delta's was suspended after one of their pledges complained to administration that they were forced to stay up for a week straight, helping the Deltas prepare for their annual Mr. Debonair pageant.

Little wasn't a very assertive guy, but he was fat, and you could tell he had some type of moxy to him, because he was far from being shy. In fact, the adjective to describe his demeanor best would probably be gregarious. But we all wear masks, so no one could have predicted the outcome of our group decision. Everyone present thought that nominating Little to be the advisor would show the school that the Bruz were moving toward a less punitive strategy of new membership selection and development.

Theodore Little was a 2000 Bruh who came into the frat via the intake program at Kappa Alpha Tau, a graduate chapter in Charlottesville, NC. He didn't pledge, but he was military, older, and an otherwise upstanding member of the community. So, the frat had to let him skate in. Little was also a reverend, so no one put up much of a fuss when he nominated himself as undergraduate advisor, assuming his goal was to do good. In hindsight, the fact he self-nominated alone should have excluded him from participating in undergraduate affairs, but the Bruz were convinced that adding a reverend to the mix would give them something close to papal sanction of their more nefarious activities. Little did anyone know that Little had his own agenda for wanting to be the undergraduate advisor. During his tenure, Little used the frat as his own personal ATM. Every piece of currency that touched Teddy's hands was funneled into the garter of Millie, a forty-something stripper at the Foxy Lady gentleman's club on Hwy. 29.

Theodore was 36 when he entered the fraternity, so his motivations for joining a college fraternity always seemed a little odd and should have been a red flag. He wasn't seeking to re-live his college youth, or necessarily desirous of running the frat. His motivations were something different, a little more overtly carnal. Despite Theodore's vows to his wife and the church, Teddy couldn't stay away from the ladies, and he knew that if there was one thing the Bruz attracted, it was the ladies. The looser the dress, the looser Teddy was with his behavior. Of course, decorum, and the need to keep earning a steady paycheck, kept Teddy in check enough for him to be a "functioning" sex-o-holic, but beyond the threshold of brazen hedonism, Teddy's life was wide open to secular speculation.

Of course, none of us knew this until after the fact, because Little didn't really hang out with the Bruz outside of meetings, but we all found out soon enough, the hard way. Two weeks into the "official" intake process of the '01 Bruz, Nationals called Darryl Rivers, the president of the graduate chapter, to tell him that the money orders for the new members had gone missing, and that all fees for initiation must be turned in with the candidates' application materials in order for them to go over. Rivers immediately contacted Little, who was the Brother responsible for mailing off all of the new initiates' application materials. At first, Little claimed that he didn't know what had happened to the money orders, but an investigation by the Grad chapter found that the money orders had been cashed by Little. Fortunately, Rivers had the foresight to require all the initiates to photocopy their money orders before submitting them to Little. A trace of the serial numbers on the money orders found out that all seven were cashed at various check cashing businesses in Salisbury. When asked to account for his actions, Little produced seven new money orders that he said he found "lost" in his personal files. Although he couldn't account for the difference in serial numbers between the newly discovered money orders and the photocopied money orders, Little was honorable enough to resign from both his posts as advisor and campus minister. He transferred his pastorate during the middle of that semester as well. Shortly after Little's resignation, I was made chapter advisor.

HOMECOMING

irty Red's plan seemed easy but pledging at Lambda Gamma was never easy: for the pledger, or the pledge. LG has a simple format, but at every step, human error abounds. Every fall the chapter begins its weed-out sessions for its spring line of pledges. Each year a new crop of eager sophomores pops up, hounding individual members of the organization as soon as school starts, asking what the necessary requirements are for entrance into the frat. Most Bruz take casual note of an aspirant's interest, fill them in on the G.P.A. and community service requirements, and (if the aspirant is lucky) they inform them to have upwards of $500 readily available to pay intake fees. At LG, expressing interest is preferred during an aspirant's freshman year, because it gives the Bruz more time to learn who the aspirant is. Plus, freshman year is when a man does most of his fucking up in college. Although a fuckup won't necessarily be held against a man trying to get into the frat, a pattern of fuckups may be suggestive of a faulty character, so freshman aspirants are to be watched over vigilantly. In a perfect world, the brother watching over the aspirant becomes a mentor to him. Watching over him, teaching him the ropes of college, and helping him graduate, even if he never joins the fraternity. Of course, things don't always run perfectly, the relationship can go the other way, and the aspirant simply turns into a sycophant, trying to admire their way into the frat, catering to the ego of exploitative Bruz. These are the type of aspirants that wind up getting used by Bruz. There are many aspirants who don't show themselves until sophomore, junior year, or (God forbid) senior year, but it is safe to say that the culture of Black Greekdom at LG favors long-term tracking in its new membership classes.

At any rate, during homecoming week, all men who have expressed interest in the organization and wish to be invited to the membership selection meeting in the spring are required to assist the Bruz with setting up for homecoming. During Homecoming, the Bruz hierarchy works like this. Old heads run the neo's, and the neo's run the GDI's (Got Damn Invidividuals). In a perfect world, the frat's pecking order would work like this all the time, but things being what they are, LG only conforms to this structure during large events like homecoming and Mardi Gras. In the absence of neo's, the youngest Bruz on the yard serve as the go-betweens between the initiated and uninitiated until pledge season rolls around. After homecoming, a watch list is maintained of all non- Bruh participants. From this list a group of letters is delivered prior to the chapter's interest meeting in November. This letter instructs its addressee, where to meet after the formal interest meeting.

At the formal interest meeting, attendees are introduced to the chapter members and the national intake committee members. They are told of the organization's history, and current community service projects. They are told that if they are interested in joining they must meet national and chapter G.P.A. requirements, pay all local, regional, and national dues up front, and be in good academic, financial, and disciplinary standing with the school. Everyone in attendance is reminded that they have not been formally offered entrance into the fraternity, but that if the fraternity should decide to offer them the privilege of membership, to remain secretive of all they've experienced.

After the meeting, those that have gotten letters meet up at the pre-determined remote location. They are finally introduced to the men who will participate in the fight club with them. They are also introduced to the core group of Bruz who are going to be pledging them.

Dirty Red, and all the other Bruz are in an uproar because, as yet, we have not found a suitable dean for the 2010 line. Normally, I'd do it, just for the sake of doing it, but, as advisor, my goal is to stay as far away from that aspect of the business as possible. I've learned through hard-fought experience that it does no one in the frat any good to have too much power consolidated in the hands of one man. Besides, being the Dean and the Advisor, takes away the plausible deniability that has been my saving grace all of these years. Normally, I can say that I'm uninvolved in undergraduate affairs, but that's hard to do when your name is all over the official paperwork.

THE FIGHT CLUB

According to common Bruh wisdom, "every man's pledge process is different," but, in my opinion, this fact is true only up to a point. There is a certain commonality to everyone's pledge process. I can't quite put my finger on it, but if there wasn't, pledging wouldn't be such a central concern of all Black Greek Organizations. At any rate, rather than narrate every pledge process that I've participated in, I'll give you folks a glimpse into the process of my favorite LG line, Spring 2004, the Imperfect Ten. Their line consisted of: Justin McLain, the ace; Ivan Adams, the deuce; Erick Hunt, the trey; Carlos Ramierez, the four; Preston Anderson, the five; Shawn Black, the six; Rodney Saunders, the seven; Fred Johnson, the eight; Vincent "Trife" Tucker, the nine; and James "Franchise" Charles, the number ten.

Their line was memorable because of the internal and external struggle we went through to get them over. That was the last line that I was personally Dean over. I have been the Dean of five of the last ten successive lines to come through Salisbury, both grad and undergraduate. In Bruh parlance, that is a legendary feat. From about spring of 2001 to spring 2005, I put hands on just about every Bruh who came through Salisbury. I felt, at that time that, since pledging didn't seem to be going anywhere anytime soon, it may as well be done correctly, and who better to do it than me, who had been baptized into it "the right way." At LG, our motto is "once you put hands on a man, it is your duty to do everything in your power to get him across the burning sands." ("Crossing The Burning Sands" means getting into the organization.) The young Bruz are so close to me because I've personally piloted most of them, not only into the fraternity, but also into a preliminary understanding of their primal manhood. At no time in recent Bruh history can I say that the chapter motto was more applicable than the 2003-2004 school year. Limestone College was being particularly vigilant during that year.

After homecoming and the interest meeting, we had the prospective candidates meet us at a middle-school football field, and then made them follow us in their cars to "the hole." The hole was our designated in-door pledge spot, sometimes affectionately dubbed "The Dog House." The place was really Brother Jeff Roberts's 18x18 tool shed during regular daytime hours. But during pledge season, after 9:00p.m., Jeff's shed turned into the war room. Sometimes, the war room stayed open until 5 a.m. We called it the hole, because once you got in it, it was hard to get out. Especially, on those "long" nights when the old head Bruz come from out of town to "bless" the next line coming through. Some nights, "Fire in the hole," is all you would hear in the shed for hours as human flesh came into contact with a wooden paddle. It was kind of funny to watch the movement of the little building from the outside. All you could hear in the tiny, wooded corner of Jeff's three acre lot, where the shed is located, was the sound of boots shuffling, bodies being thrown up against walls, and the exhausted whispers of worn-out soldiers. I remember clearly what was going on when the trouble for the '04's began.

Carlos, the #4 pledge on the line, who was also the first Mexican student to try to get down at Limestone, was having his night. He was an acting student and played the part of the dedicated student to a tee. But Jeff discovered a chink in his armor on his last weekly visit to the school to check up on the potentials' academic progress. Jeff, who was a bail bondsman and detective, checked grades habitually, as a matter of duty. Over the years, it has become imperative to the Bruz that candidates remain in good academic standing during the process because we don't want school officials saying that the fraternity is an academic hindrance to its members. On the contrary, the Bruz consider themselves academic motivators.

Dr. Rhoda Starks, an AKA, and director of the college's theatre department, reported to Jeff on the sly that Carlos had missed two important class sessions, and had not as yet performed his qualifying monolog for the department. According to her, Carlos was more concerned about his extra-curricular life than his curricular life. She said she understood what Carlos might be going through, since she pledged at Morgan State in '81, but that Carlos had a responsibility to himself to take his academic potential to the next level, even if his fraternal aspirations would have to suffer because of it.

Jeff was incensed! No pledge underneath him was going to be a dummy. Dr. Starks was a nosey busy-body, but she was also an accurate barometer of public sentiment toward the Bruz. She'd spent half her life more concerned with what the Bruz where doing, than most of the Bruz were concerned over what the Bruz were doing. She could (and would) tell you the exact character and demeanor of every Bruh that ever walked on

Limestone's campus from 1985 until now. Although she would never admit to smashing one of the Bruz, she most certainly couldn't deny her unnatural preoccupation with the men of the fraternity – Jeff, in particular. So, it is safe to say that she wasn't lying or idly gossiping when she dropped a dime on Carlos. He was one of her favorite students, she said, but no one should be allowed to skirt the Black Greek rule of personal responsibility. Public notoriety has its pitfalls, and Carlos was about to find what one of those pitfalls were.

I didn't find out about the Carlos thing until later that night. I'd had a long day at the library, so I wasn't really paying close attention to the pledges or the Bruz that night. The boys were in the hole with their assistant Dean, Jonathan "Mud" Ross. He was warming them up for a visit with some of the older chapter Bruz. The line was rehearsing the poems and fraternity history we taught them. If they successfully passed their test of bravery tonight, they would move on to the next stage of their initiation process, and we would begin to teach them the basics of how to step. I stood outside the hole that night smoking, watching the stars, drifting off. But, right before I could light up another one, I saw Jeff marching towards me, huffing and puffing so hard he looked like a bull in full charge.

I said, "What's up Jeff?" But, he just blew right past me without a word. When he swung the door to the hole open, I rushed in behind him to make sure none of us caught a charge. I could tell he was mad. But I wasn't sure if it was genuine anger, or a ploy to keep the potentials on-guard. Jeff grabbed the two-foot paddle we call, "Little

Ax", from off the wall as soon as he entered. He made everybody stop what they were doing, and sit down, except Carlos, so that he could have the floor.

"This muthaucka number four thinks he's gonna charm his way into the frat, like he's frickin' Ricky Valentino, without putting in any work!" Everybody in the room was baffled, but spellbound, because Carlos was a good kid, and Jeff was usually one of the quietest Bruz in the grad chapter. "I'm on the yard today and his got- damn teacher pulls me to the side and tells me she doesn't think he's ready to be in the frat because he's already letting it get in the way of his studies." Carlos was a deer caught in the headlights. "This Nigga ain't been going to class, is missing assignments, making excuses, and…" I cut Jeff off, motioning to him to stop with my right hand.

"Is this true number four?" Before he could speak, I yelled, "Fuck that, I don't want to know if it's true or not! I frankly don't give a shit either way. But I do give a shit that this type of negative shit is being said about you. If it weren't true, your name wouldn't even be involved in that type of conversation." I addressed everyone in the room, "As a Bruh, academics should never be a question. Academics are why we are here in college. Your studies now, shape the terrain of your life in the future. If you don't gain anything from this fraternity other than this lesson, get it, and get it good. The Bruz are an extra- curricular activity that promotes scholarship. We are NOT an organization of shirt wearers, who are banned together for no other reason than to enjoy the company of our selves. If you can't cut the mustard in class, why the fuck are you donating your free-time to hanging with the frat? This is not a street gang. We're not a bunch of hoodlums who are hanging out on the corner for lack of something better to do with ourselves. If that's why any of you are here, NOW, is the time for you to find the door. I'm not in the business of validating dummies." No one took their eyes off of me, except for Carlos, who must have been trying to find an excuse for his actions somewhere on the floor because he didn't look up until Jeff open-hand smacked him on the back of the neck so hard Carlos stood up at attention with his eyes facing an imaginary spot on the ceiling from that point on when the Bruz were talking to him.

As a punishment for Carlos's transgression, I taught his line a lesson on laziness. I had them line up for an exercise I like to call "Machine Gun Funk." During Machine Gun Funk, each man, in order of smallest to tallest, takes one stroke of wood, in a constant rotation until the five to ten Bruz swinging wood get tired. Normally, I set a limit on how much wood any line can take during a set because I don't want us to leave too many bruises, or cause permanent damage to anyone's ass. But this was one of those "let it ride" teaching moments I talked about earlier. First, I sat Carlos to the side and made him watch his LB's get pummeled for fifty minutes. Mud, Jeff, Dirty Red, Tiny, and Tito ('99 LG) were swinging wood. Of all the Bruz, Tito had the worst swing because he was a tennis coach.

When we finished with them, not only was Carlos sorry that his group was being punished for what he'd done (or didn't do, in this case), but his LB's were mad at him for having to be tortured for his laziness. The lesson being taught was that everyone suffers when one person fails to do his job. While his LB's where getting thrashed, Carlos was made to lie on his stomach, not letting it touch the ground, in push-up position, keeping his head up facing his line brothers during their wood session.

One of the Bruz, "Stink Rat," was in Carlos's ear the whole time singing "Lift Every Voice and Sing." Don't ask me why Stink Rat was singing the national anthem, but he was, and it wasn't harming anything, so I allowed it.

When we finished with the line, we made all of them get into push-up position and singled Carlos out. His version of Machine gun funk was to take a stroke of wood from each Bruh swinging, jump up and say "thank you for making me into a scholar," run around in a circle as if he was getting to the back of a line and moving up to the front again, and then get right back down in his wood taking stance to start the rotation all over again. After an hour, I sat him down, and recited these words to him taught to me by one of the '86 LG Bruz, Greg "Root" Cosby:

The Black Greek experience serves as a catalyst for self-actualization, personal motivation, and high scholastic achievement. Without these, we are nothing; with these, we have the potential to be any and every thing we choose.

Carlos was crying, but I stood him up again, by himself, with the rest of the group sitting in a semi-circle around him watching, and made him learn the poem right then and there. He had to learn to say the poem from memory, so I didn't let his LB's help him learn it. Every time he would mess up he was given a choice of a stroke of wood or do twenty push-ups. "There are always consequences for not studying Carlos," I told him. By 12:30a.m. he had done 160 push up, and was teaching the poem to his LB's.

Around 1a.m. that night, Darryl Rivers, who was just elected as the Grad Chapter President at the time, but was acting as the advisor even though he didn't work on campus, came into the hole to tell me that Nationals sent a letter to his office and told us to shut our process down. They had gotten word from school officials that Lambda Gamma had been reported for hazing so they were sending out an investigator to "clear things up, and get to the bottom of any wrongdoing that may have occurred."

2-7-04

Dear Brother Rivers,

It has come to our attention that there has been a violation of the fraternity's hazing policy within your jurisdiction. As a matter of procedure, we are sending a member of the fraternity's regional intake team to investigate. At this time it is your duty to inform all undergraduate members, and perspective initiates, that the membership intake process for the fraternity is ceased until further notice. Furthermore, a full investigation of this matter, that absolves the fraternity of any criminal negligence or wrongdoing, will be conducted. Any members found in violation of the fraternity's "No Hazing" policy will be punished to the fullest extent of the law. Please refer to your "Fraternity Advisor's Manual" for further guidance in proceeding with this matter. If you have any further questions on this matter, please contact Bro. Raymond Bradshaw at: 704-595-7629.

Fraternally Yours, Bro. Miller Fox

Darryl didn't really have to read the letter to me. The fact that the letter existed was proof enough, for me, that we were all in hot water. After we shut down the war room that night, I couldn't get the look of distress on everyone's faces out of my mind. It finally dawned on me that these Bruz had wives and kids, jobs and futures. Not to mention the potentials. How would they react to the process being suspended? How were any of us going to explain to the world that we went to jail for some shit like pledging?

Darryl wanted me to know what was going on because, although the letter was addressed to him, as acting advisor, he had to tell Nationals that he'd passed the advisorship over to me because he wasn't qualified. In reality, Darryl was politely scooting himself away from the situation. But, since I was the Dean of the line, and an employee of the college, I decided to man-up, and take the reigns of leadership for this case. Besides, since I was obviously going to be implicated in whatever nonsense that had been told to Nationals, I wanted to at least try to be the master of my fate. With good reason, I didn't trust all the Bruz to maintain their silence and solidarity during this new ordeal.

THE GRAD BRUZ

There have always been two types of Graduate Bruz in the frat, those that pledged undergrad and those that didn't. Of those that didn't, some "pledge" the grad chapter, some don't, it really just depends on what the culture of the Grad chapter is like. The relationship between the Grad Bruz that pledged undergrad and the ones that didn't gets kind of dicey at times. For one, those Grad Bruz that pledged undergrad, feel a certain sense of superiority amongst all the Bruz in general (and the grad Bruz specifically) because they've not only pledged, but they've also remained an active financial member of the organization well into their adult years. Those that didn't pledge undergrad, on the other hand, feel a certain stigmatism within the frat because, if they are young and pledge grad, they're probably doing so only because they were rejected during undergrad; and if they are old, they're constantly being questioned about why "after all these years" do they want to join a college fraternity? Added to the complexity of this situation is the fact that after a man has lived a certain number of years, he's hard to change, and transition into the strange pecking order of the Bruz isn't the easiest of fits for men stuck in their ways.

More than one or two fights have broken out at the plot over the difference between Bruh culture and regular culture.

Grad Bruz play a pivotal position within the fraternity because (ultimately) within the corporate structure of the fraternity they "handle all the business" of the organization. The business carried out by most graduate chapters is functionary: visible community service, hosting public events in the organizations name, correspondence with national headquarters, etc., etc. Since about the mid-90's, however, graduate chapters have become even more powerful in the fraternity because Nationals gave them the authority to manage the local undergraduate intake process. The theory behind this decision was that graduate brothers are usually older than undergrads, and henceforth, more mature in their decision-making processes. But conventional wisdom doesn't always reign in the frat. One reason for this, especially when it comes to intake, is that being older in physically chronological age doesn't necessarily mean that a man is older than another man in fraternally chronological age. Nor does being physically older than another man mean that one brother has more insight into the inner-workings of the fraternity than the other. For instance, say a man pledged when he was twenty, and has been in the frat for seven years. In frat years, he is older than a man of forty, who has been in the frat for only one year and should know better how to conduct the business of the organization. This may sound like semantics, but these types of anomalies do happen in the frat, and in fact, cause great tension within the folds.

During the '04 pledge process Bro. Darwin "Do More" Spears proved this. I didn't know it then, but when I was nominated for Intake chairman at the October grad chapter meeting, Spears was attempting a subtle coup of not only the intake process, but the entire fraternity in Rowan County as well. Apparently, Spears was the Bruh who initially nominated me for the intake chair position because, according to him, I was "one of the only Bruz in Rowan County with any sense." His goal was to do away with the process totally, underground and above-ground. My decline of the nomination temporarily thwarted his plans, and instantly put me on his to do list. But it wasn't until after Teddy Little got suspended, and Darryl Rivers handed the advisorship over to me, that I had to come face-to-face with the warped individualism that resided within the heart (if that's what it can be said to be: a heart, that is) of old Do More Spears.

I went to Teddy's house to talk with him the day after I found out about the investigation. Apparently, it was Spears who told the school to watch us. He had since been contacted by the fraternity for a statement, but he refused, telling them he'd only talk to them if a national representative of the fraternity was present face-to-face. "You never know who you can trust in the frat, I need to see a man's eyes to know if he's being honest with me or not."

"I detest the thought of young men suffering," were his first words to me. "What Lambda Gamma has going on isn't a pledge process, it's a torture session. And since it doesn't teach aspirants anything other than violence, I want it stopped. I've seen several lines come through Salisbury, grad and undergrad, since I've been over. But never, in any of them, not even one of them, have I seen the type of men our fraternity says it wants to attract. In fact, we're regressing. We're trampling the ideals of the fraternity under the foot of our own refusal to elevate our moral character. It's as if the Bruz are scared to do away with the thug nigga image. Instead of being great, we hope for mediocre."

I listened patiently as he soliloquized his philosophy on the frat. I was careful not to say too much in his house, because I felt as if anything I said could and would be used against me in a court of law.

"Let your 'yeses' be 'yeses' and your 'no's' be 'no's' Fierce," were his last words to me before I was asked to leave without getting a chance to say my piece. I assumed that this was the main point of his lecture.

Spears was 56 years old, but he'd only been in the frat four years. In those four years, he'd gotten it into his head that the only thing that the frat was missing was his influence. In 2000, he tried unsuccessfully to be nominated as undergraduate advisor. In 2001, he tried unsuccessfully to oust Bro. Eric "Show Time" Frazier as the grad chapter president, claiming him "procedurally incompetent." And in 2002, he finally succeeded in being nominated as Chapter Secretary, but was soon ousted himself for ruining the entire graduate process. Spears used his position as chapter secretary to "accidentally" misplace some of the Chapter's intake information. Although the missing documents were found, the deadline for their submission had passed, so the Grad Chapter had to wait another semester for intake. Spears escaped formal chapter retribution because nationals determined that it wasn't "totally" his fault that the deadline was missed. Bro. Raymond Bradshaw, the Regional Intake Chairman for North and South Carolina, was late corresponding with Spears about the deadlines. The Bruz in the chapter took exception, however, to the fact that the only misplaced transcripts were those of the applicants Spears thought most objectionable. According to Raymond Bradshaw "this is a common mistake, and a brother cannot be formally sanctioned for carelessness, only privately criticized." His suggestion to us was to change

Chapter Secretaries at the next elections and try again with this same group of aspirants next year. We did just that, fortunately, but it caused a heck of a lot of confusion in both the undergrad and graduate chapters because we had to re-schedule graduate intake for the following fall, rather than the summer when we normally take them over. Everything worked out for the best though because the fall '02 graduate chapter line got a chance to be pledged by all the old school Bruz that came to homecoming that year. Not to mention, we got to use the graduate line's labor, in addition to the undergrads and their aspirants, to ensure that homecoming '02 was the greatest Bruh event in history. Bro. Frazier made a formal motion in the meeting right after '02 went over to keep Spears away from the intake process because "his assistance had been proven detrimental to the growth of the fraternity." It was seconded, but not passed.

That following spring, Spears was madder than ever at the Bruz. It took him a whole extra year to exact his revenge, but when he the call to the school reporting our undergrad process came through, I knew exactly what had precipitated his betrayal. It was technically Thursday morning when we found out that nationals had us under investigation, but the chain of events that caused this interruption started the previous Monday of that very same week. Apparently, among his many other gripes with the Bruz, Spears felt especially slighted from the '04 undergrad process because no one would tell him anything about it. In fact, to say the Bruz froze him out is an understatement. We down-right blackballed him. The old head LG Bruz who were active members in the

Salisbury graduate chapter even made a pact amongst themselves that they would not mention the undergrad process in their meetings to prevent Spears from "fouling things up."

In response to this slight Spears appealed directly to me, the soon-to-be reluctant advisor.

"What's going on with the undergrads Fierce," he asked, in a voice half-order, half-complaint. He cornered me on campus the Friday before his call to administration. His eyebrows were furrowed, and his bald head was shining with perspiration.

"Nothing much," was my response. I hoped to appear casual, so we could keep the conversation breezy, and not talk about the 400-pound elephant in the room. He knew I was lying, of course, but as a graduate Bruh, who never pledged at Limestone, he knew he didn't have the privilege of digging too deeply into the internal affairs of the undergraduate chapter. Spears did try to pledge undergrad once when he was in college, but he dropped due to injuries he suffered during the process. In his mind, this fact alone gave him some quasi-moral right to know what was going on with Lambda Gamma. In my mind, an opposing idea was formulating. As the current Resident Hall Director at Limestone, Spearman was far too close to administration for me to be comfortable letting him involve himself in affairs he had no business being in. As advisor, I had a duty to ALL the Bruz on campus to keep them safe from harm.

"You're lying to me," he said. "You and all the other Bruz are trying to freeze me out because I won't play the game." True, on every count, but it wasn't my place to tell him.

"What game?" I asked innocently.

"You know what game I'm talking about. This pledging thing in Salisbury has to stop, immediately. Not only is it contradictory to the stated goals of the fraternity. I think that it inspires an unwanted thuggery in the new young men that come in that is downright cancerous. We're trying to develop leaders, not create brutes and slaves." Spears always handled confrontation with indignation. "If nothing is going on now, it soon will be, and if I find out about it, it won't be for long."

"Is that a threat or a promise?" I asked. I had to say something, even though I had nothing to say.

"Don't trifle with me Fierce," he had to lower his voice because he didn't want it to look like we were two staff members arguing in public. (Not that that would have raised too many eyebrows at Limestone.) He continued in a more muffled tone, "I know the Bruz think that I'm trying to sabotage the process, and take over the grad chapter, but I'm not. I am only doing what we're all supposed to be doing: being a leader. The founders were not barbarians, and neither should we be. But the Bruz around here act as if a non-barbarian method of doing things doesn't exist." He had a very valid point – but, so.

I interjected. "It's not that a softer way of doing things doesn't exist, Darwin, it's just that the softer way doesn't work to produce anything worthwhile." I did a quick survey of the scene to make sure no one was watching us. "If these dudes were coming into the frat just to learn Robert's Rules of Order, they would do better by joining the local Elks Club or the Chamber of Commerce. Joining the frat is about pledging, bottom line, and you know it, Darwin."

"And beating these boys half to death teaches them what about leadership, Fierce?" He had me stumped and he knew it. "I want to know who is on this upcoming line, and I want to know now." The look in his eyes was designed to be threatening, but beyond his glare, I could see the intractable arrogance of a man so stuck in his ways that working with others for a common goal was damn near impossible for him to fathom.

"Not gonna happen Darwin," I told him confidently. "The frat is a business, but it ain't the Civitan Club, some company policies aren't really up for revision just because market conditions change. You'll see who is on the line when everybody else does," I said this to place him on the same level as all other outsiders. He knew it and was infuriated.

"Oh, so the Bruz are gonna treat me like a GDI, huh? Well, if that's the case, I'm going to act like a GDI then too. Don't let me find out about a line, 'cause there for sure won't be no line when I get through wit' y'all." And with that, he turned his back to me, with his right index finger still waving in the sky. You could see him cussing out loud to himself all the way down to hill to his office in the dormitory. Students covered their giggling mouths with one hand as they watched the always cool and collected Spears ranting to himself about something unknown.

He made good on his threat too. That weekend he pumped every student living in the dorms that he could for information on who was pledging the Bruz that year. By Sunday, he had just about everyone's name, but he was only able to catch #'s 2, 5, and 8. They all lived on campus in the residence halls.

Monday morning, he called them into his office to quiz them about their fraternal aspirations. It was impossible for them to lie to him about their desire to join the fraternity because they had to get his signature to show the frat that they were in good standing with residence life on campus. They did, however, lie through their teeth about being hazed or pledging that semester. He expected this. "We've never been hazed as far as we know" was all any one of them would say about it.

Even though Spears was 56 years old, and Grad, he pledged in Salisbury in 1999, so he knew how the Bruz operated. He also knew how pledges operated, and that a little fear and intimidation could go a long way toward getting you what you want. "I know that you gentleman h ave been given instructions not to talk to anyone about your pledge process." He greeted them. "The Bruz may have even told you not to talk to me specifically about it," they all shook their heads feigning shock and disbelief at his accusations. "I don't care about any of that. The reason I called you three here is to give you a chance to get into the fraternity legitimately."

Legitimately, they all wondered what this meant. They were under the impression that pledging was "the right way" to get into the frat because they'd all heard about the sucky frat experiences of friends, they'd known who went paper in other organizations. They chose to pledge the Bruz, primarily, because the Bruz still pledged, and everybody knew it. "No sense in doing something if you're going to do it half-assed," is what their Assistant Dean, Mud, used say all the time.

"Did you know that Lambda Gamma hasn't sent any paperwork to nationals concerning you? Or that, in the past the chapter has pledged guys for entire semesters and never actually turned them into legitimate Bruz?" Spears could see their insecurities getting the best of them. "What makes you think that they are really going to take you guys over? They're just stringing you guys along so that you'll keep running around at their beckon call." Spears was a snake, and a shrewd one at that. He'd caught the potentials early enough in the process to still be able to play on their mistrust and self-doubt. He was right about most of what he was saying, but wrong for using the same tactics against them, that he claimed he was trying to prevent us from using, namely, hazing. In this case Spears was using the mental, rather than the physical kind of hazing, but it was hazing nonetheless. Especially when he told them, "The only way you guys are going to get into this fraternity is through me, and if you want my cooperation, you'll have to cooperate with me." Their fate was sealed.

THE PLEDGEE

E ver since he can remember Ivan wanted to be the Bruz. His dad was a Bruh. His uncles were Bruz, and his favorite teacher in high school was one too. Hell, his girlfriend was even joining a sorority to be closer to him once he became a Bruh. When he came to college the first organization he looked up was the Bruz. His freshman year, he worshipped them as much as one man should another. He even spent his after-class hours in the library, getting his GPA up so that sophomore year he could "get on line" to become the Bruz. Fortunately, fall semester of his sophomore year he was in English class with Jeremy "Light Bright" Randall. Randall told him that he had to get to know the Bruz. To do this Randall and two other guys who expressed interest in the fraternity were invited to attend a fraternity party. But rather than enjoy the party as normal guests, the three gentlemen along with four young men they had never met acted as butlers the entire party. Although not formally offered membership into the organization on this night, it was fully understood by all involved that there was a certain protocol that must be followed in order to become worthy of joining the fight club. Light Bright never explained to Ivan what line was going to be like, but on the one occasion

Ivan did muster up the courage to ask him directly, Light Bright answered cryptically: "He who is humble is confident and wise. He who brags is insecure and lacking."

Ivan never understood what that meant, but it was all he could think of sitting in the hot seat of Reverend Spears' office. His shame-faced LB's didn't seem to be fairing too well either. None of them really said too much, and they all spent more time looking at the floor than at the old man who was standing before them trying to kill their dreams. Ivan sure wished that Light Bright, or one of the other Bruz he'd been seeing during the fight club for the past three weeks was there to tell them how to answer Spears' questions. They had been warned about talking to administration, but they were also warned not to ignore the Bruz either. Spears was both, so which side of him should they listen to? Both halves of him were saying the same thing: "Are you pledging?" Maybe Spears was trying to trick them into giving up a false confession, and once given, he'd run back and tell the Bruz they were snitches, and they'd get thrashed. Or even worse, maybe the Bruz were trying to see who the week link on the line was, and if they told, they'd never get a chance to go over. But then again, what if Spears wasn't fooling and they all got kicked out of school for not telling him that they were trying to join the frat?

"Sir," Ivan said, addressing Rev. Spears. The Bruz had taught him and his LB's to always address a Bruh as "sir," it was easy to remember with Spears because he always acted like a "sir." "We all are very interested in joining your fraternity, but none of us have been harmed in the slightest by any members of your organization." Internally, Ivan was hoping his flimsy excuse worked. Of course, it didn't.

"Is that a fact," Spears smiled as he edged closer to the seated young men. Spears smiling meant trouble. It meant he was either masking his anger, or showing off his fangs before he struck. "Then you gentleman won't mind me taking pictures of you, so that we can document the fact that none of you have been harmed in the slightest way by anybody…" He had them trapped.

Ivan knew what pictures meant. He'd heard about his friend Ben who got caught trying to pledge a fraternity two years ago at Albany State. Administrators at Ben's school subjected his line to a full-body search and used the bruises on their butts and backs as evidence against the fraternity and the pledges. All of the Bruz on the yard at Albany were kicked out of school, and none of the pledges got to go over undergrad - ever.

"Don't worry," Spears said. "I'm not going to get you all kicked out of school, so long as you help me. In fact, I'll make sure you all get into the frat. But first, I am going to get to the bottom of this pledging business at this school, and I will stop it by hook or crook."

Spears told the potentials that their meeting could be a secret between the four of them, and the potentials all agreed that it was best if they did. When Ivan broke down that night after set and told me what happened I told him that I didn't think it was a major incident, and simply charged it to Spears trying to impose his personal will on the frat again. I was more shocked than I should have been two days later when I found out the full extent of the secret meeting between Spears and the potentials.

Spears took pictures of the potentials and sent them to the Director of Student Activities and the President of the college, along with a letter accusing the Bruz (some by name) of "pledging these students with no concern for the safety and well-being of these impressionable young men, or care for the sanctity of the fraternity."

THE ADMINISTRATORS

The letter and pictures were pretty damaging evidence, to say the least, but since I was the advisor, and one of the names specifically mentioned in the incident, it was up to me to make this case go away. Why should I, or anybody for that fact, lose their life, freedom, and reputation for something so silly as hazing? I kept reciting my favorite stanza from the poem "See It Through" by Edgar Guest on the walk over to the President's office from the library. The Bruz taught me that poem while I was on line, and it was always my solace during troubled times.

> When you're up against a trouble,
> Meet it squarely, face to face;
> Lift your chin and set your shoulders,
> Plant your feet and take a brace.
> When it's vain to try to dodge it,
> Do the best that you can do;
> You may fail, but you may conquer,
> See it through!

I had to answer my accusers face-to-face. The school gave me a chance to even before I had an opportunity to prepare myself. In a letter placed on my desk Thursday afternoon, I was summonsed to President Johnson's office Friday morning for a meeting with him, the fraternity's regional intake chairman, and the Director of Student Affairs, Dr. Erick Jackson. President Johnson I'd met before, and Bradshaw had proven himself time-and- time again a pompous boob. Jackson, however, I didn't know much about. But I knew that he didn't like me. Office water cooler talk was that he thought I thought too much of myself. "Chance is all warp and no woof," is how Mrs. Frost, the security guard at the front booth of the college, put it. Jackson was President Johnson's right-hand man when it came to student-related issues. Their policy was to "keep everything in-house" as much as possible, except in cases of hazing. Jackson and Spears, because of the nature of their departments, knew each other well and saw eye to eye on a number of issues, especially pledging. I wouldn't necessarily call them friends, but their weird type of work politics, tends to form unholy strategic alliances during times of mutual danger or opportunity. Hazing was a hot-button issue even in white society, so the school thought it best to adopt a pro-active stance in these types of matters whenever it looked as if public attention might be thrust upon the school. Jackson's opinion would weigh heavily on the President's view of this case. My only chance was to make the accusations look false, or at least flimsy, which was a long shot.

Although the meeting was being billed as a preliminary investigation, I knew that if I didn't play my cards right that it was going to be a preliminary sentencing. The next meeting would involve the law, and that's never good. If we were at a traditionally white institution this case might be a little more easily navigated because TWI's are much less familiar with the dynamics of how Black Greek Organizations operate internally. Nobody really gives a hoot what the coloreds do to each other, just so long as they don't kill one another or damage property. But at an HBCU, Black Greeks are a central concern of everybody, and campus scandals are what make the world go 'round. If this particular scandal went any farther than it already had, I would be looking for a new job and a good lawyer faster than I could say "I didn't do it."

What I had working for me was that Spears had never actually been to set himself, and that none of the potentials gave him any details of the bruises and scars on their bodies. Ivan said that Spears wanted them to sign affidavits explaining the marks, but he backed down to their protests when Fred, the #8, said that he refused to sign anything without an attorney. Fred was a Criminal Justice major and knew enough about the law to talk about his rights, so Spears let them leave his office, but warned them that it might be in their best interest to get a lawyer.

What I didn't have working for me was that Spears was a reverend and respected administrator at the college. Not to mention the fact that he was a highly respected member of the Salisbury community in general. Even before the frat, Spears was a leader among leaders. The fact that he had pictures of the potentials bruised body parts, and was a member of the organization, seemed to ensure that Darwin Spears had finally won his long-time battle against pledging. His only adversary in this contest was the people he was accusing. It seemed he was about to claim the game, the set, and the match.

The only thing I could do when I got into President Johnson's office was tell the truth about the Fight Club as best I could when asked to give my account of the situation. President

Johnson's secretary, Margaret Marvell, a Delta, made me wait in the lobby of his office before the meeting began. Waiting there, I realized that the high ceilings, wood-paneled walls, austere pictures, and imposing furniture strewn about the room, were all designed to intimidate, as well as comfort, guests visiting the President. I wondered if I was being made to wait in the lobby to scare me into confessing my transgressions. I kept steeling my reserve with my poem.

> Black may be the clouds about you
> And your future may seem grim,
> But don't let your nerve desert you;
> Keep yourself in fighting trim.
> If the worst is bound to happen,
> In spite of all that you can do,
> Running from it will not save you,
> See it through!

I was allowed to enter the office after Jackson entered the waiting room. He tipped his hat at me smiling, "Good day, Chance," but didn't stop long enough to shake the right hand I was about to extend to him. He blew right by me into the President's office. "You can go in now." Margaret pointed her finger at the door to signal me, as if I needed directions.

The stuffy décor of the lobby was a precursor to the stuffy décor of President Johnson's interior office. You would think the guy was President of an English yachting club, instead of a southern HBCU. But it was laid out. With more books than even I could read. I was shocked to see Bradshaw already in the office before even Jackson or me. He was comfortably seated in the President's winged queen chair in the corner behind his own wing- back desk chair. In typical Bradshaw fashion, he was monitoring the cistern of Brandy near the alcove window, so he didn't pay much attention to me or Jackson when we came in. He was in the middle of one of his war stories, and President Johnson was spell-bound.

"So anyways, me and the Bruz come out the girl's room, and Walter "Sweet-back" Jenkins says he got to go back in because he left the watch his old lady gave him…" He had to pause because his laughter caused a slight wheeze that made him double-over just enough for his drink to spill a little bit. President Johnson made things worse by smacking Bradshaw on the back, trying to gain his own composure to hear the rest of the shared memory. "Anyhow, Sweet-back wound up having to have his fiancé bail him out of jail for fighting with the prostitutes husband." The two bust into hysterics. Apparently, Bradshaw and Johnson joined the frat in the same era – Johnson at Limestone, Bradshaw at Winston- Salem State. They traveled in the same circle of Bruz since the early 70's. After a moment, they finally acknowledged our presence.

I tried to join in on the merriment to ease the tension. "Don't stop on our account. I love to listen to the older Bruz reminisce." They didn't bite.

"Long before your time Youngblood! Long Before your time…" Bradshaw said, swirling the snifter of Brandy in his right hand. He and the President chuckled to each other one more time before they prepared to get down to business. President Johnson turned back to his desk to settle down.

"Good afternoon, Gentlemen," President Johnson said.

"Good Afternoon, Sir" We both said simultaneously out of habit. Dr. Jackson took the seat in the guest chair in front of the President, to right of me. "No, no,

Jackson. Sit behind me, in the chair opposite Mr. Bradshaw. We are missing one more guest," the President said. He then added, "Where is Mr. Spears?"

"He's on his way," Jackson retorted, "He had some business to attend to in the dorms, but he told my secretary that he'd be over as soon he was finished."

"Well, we can't sit around waiting for him all day, I've got a busy schedule, so let's be on with this business. Mr. Chance, I'm sure you know why you're here…"

"In fact, I don't Sir," I had to stall him.

"You are here because Brother Spears says that you're the ringleader of an underground pledge class, does that ring a bell?" He raised his eyebrows like Sherlock Holmes after he makes a brilliant point.

"It actually doesn't. Why would he say that?"

"That's why we have brought you here, rather than dragging in all the undergrads. I know they'll all deny it, but Spears has been circulating some pretty damning pictures that I want someone to explain how he came in possession of." The President told me about the case as he knew it. "You and several members of the undergraduate chapter are currently pledging ten students four nights a week for the past four weeks." He was up from his chair now, pacing behind his desk as he talked. His head remained high in the air as he talked, as if he was reading a monologue to the ceiling. "I'm sure you're aware of the school and fraternity's zero tolerance policy when it comes to hazing. And understand that as a faculty member, your future is in grave danger if it is found that you are personally responsible for illegal activity, fraternal or otherwise." My heart dropped to my stomach.

"Yes, Sir, and I flatly deny any wrongdoing on my part." I made sure to put as much confidence in my voice as I could possibly muster.

"Well, how do you explain these pictures Spears took of three of the aspirants under your charge?"

"President Johnson, esteemed colleagues, I'm not sure what to make of this case. I've done my own investigation into the facts of this 'alleged' hazing and have come to a bit of a crossroads about the whole situation." They all stared at me in skeptical disbelief. But I had the floor, so I had to make the best of it. "What we have here is a conundrum. On the one hand, we have a respected staff and fraternity member, doing what he feels is his duty. On the other hand, we have all participants in the acts Spears alleges happened denying all of these said allegations categorically. Of course, this wouldn't be the first-time students tried to cover up a hazing incident, but I don't think that a student cover-up is exactly what is going on here. In fact, I think we are missing the forest for the trees on this one." I paused for dramatic effect. The president's secretary buzzed in before I could continue.

"Dr. Johnson, Mr. Spears is here to see you." Great. "Send him in Margaret," President Johnson said. "I invited Mr. Spears here so that we could all get to the bottom of these serious accusations."

As Spears entered the room his focus automatically shifted to me. Apparently, he was just as shocked and put off by my presence as I was to his. Both of us should have been slapped for not anticipating the obvious. Black people 101, the person that looks guiltiest usually is. President Johnson brought us together to see who was really telling the truth.

"Good afternoon gentlemen," Spears hissed in his nasally alto voice. "Forgive my tardiness, I had to conduct a room search of the third floor in one of the boys' dorms. There were reports of loud parties and marijuana smoke last night, and I thought that a room check this morning would turn up some pretty interesting results."

"Well, did you find anything?" Bradshaw asked, trying to bring himself up to speed on campus scuttle bug. He may have been asking out of genuine interest, or he may have been trying to put us all at ease with himself, so we would let our guard down during questioning.

"As a matter of fact, we did find marijuana in one student's closet, and two more had half-empty bottles of alcohol hiding under their beds." President Johnson and Dr. Jackson didn't look at all phased or impressed by Spears' report. I couldn't help but stare at the President's snifter collection while all this banter was going on. I was antsy. I felt the need to interrupt the pleasantries.

"Excuse me gentlemen, may I please continue with what I was saying?" My demeanor caught everyone off guard.

"Yes, Yes, Yes," President Johnson said, trying to regain dominance over the exchange. "Mr. Chance was explaining to us his own personal investigation into this hazing business right before you stepped in Mr. Spears." He wasn't expecting to hear that.

"I came right on time then. I have never seen a criminal investigate themselves – Outside of the government, of course." Spears had impeccable timing when it came to Black humor. He was born to be a preacher.

As annoyed as I was trying to pretend, I was at the interruptions, I was actually thankful for Spears' intrusion because it gave me time to think of what I was going to say next. A few more minutes of thinking and I believe I could have gotten the President to believe it was him who did the hazing. I began calmly:

"As I was saying, we do have a very strange case here, but I think that we are missing the forest for the trees when it comes to the facts of this case. Yes, three of our students were involved in hazing, and do have a legitimate gripe against the fraternity." Spears smiled, and Bradshaw winced, thinking about all the paperwork this impending calamity was going to cause.

"These poor kids have been drug through the mud and exploited. But it is not the accused that should stand before judgment for their mistreatment, it is their accuser, who is in the wrong." There was a million miles of silence in the room for one second as those present attempted to digest what I just said, until Spears shot up out of his seat.

"What the fuck are you talking about, Chance?" "You know what I'm talking about, Spears," I could barely keep my composure I was so excited by my own brilliance. "The only crimes committed against these young men, are the crimes committed by you. Well, except for the crime you made everyone else accessories to."

"Huh?" Jackson and Bradshaw exclaimed simultaneously. The look of bafflement around the room was absolutely exhilarating.

"It seems to me that the only crime committed was coercing those boys into letting you take naked pictures of them, and then distributing them in the mail to other people." Clearly no one had looked at things from this angle. "In fact, I'm no lawyer, but I think that since you didn't get those young men's permission to distribute their naked images through the mail, that that can be construed as forced pornography."

"That's a damn lie and you know it, Fierce!" Spears was fuming. At age 56, and weighing only a whopping 119 pounds, I don't Darwin Spears ever punched another man in his life, but the look in his eyes told me that the thought of it was milling around in his mind like a gerbil on a hamster wheel. "You aren't gonna twist this one on me, I'll sue you and the frat, and the school for liable."

"Oh really, are sure you want everyone to know how you brought up these phony accusations of hazing to cover up your own little sordid habits? How are we sure what happened to those young men's bodies? Maybe those discolorations are just make-up. I didn't see any faces, how do we know its even the people you say they are. And more importantly, why did you feel the need to take pictures as evidence anyways?"

"Okay, that's enough out of both of you," President Jackson brought his fist down hard on his desk. "I'm not buying that story either Chance, and Spears the school has more than enough money to fight the legal team you will be able assemble without a steady income. Do I make myself clear? You both better come better, or both of you two ex-employees can go home right now."

"Well Sir," I had to clean things up. "I didn't say that the aspirants haven't been doing anything?" I had to wet their appetites.

"Do tell Chance, do tell..." Spears said. "Hush Spears," President Johnson said.

"The aspirants and the undergraduates are participating in a game they like to call Fight Club."

"Fight Club?" Dr. Jackson interjected, as if the words themselves didn't make sense, let alone the combination of them.

"Yes, Fight Club. I just found out about it myself, right before Spears submitted his complaint." Plausible deniability.

"How convenient," interrupted Spears.

"The game is basically what its name implies. The participants square up against each other in a no fist brawl for two minutes a round. According to the undergraduates, wrestling is preferred, and no punches are allowed. The Lambda Gamma Bruz say they've been playing the game amongst themselves all year, and only recently decided to let the three gentlemen Spears says he took the pictures of participate. They say they thought it would be a good way for all of them to get to know one another."

"So this is how they pledge people these days?" President Johnson asked.

"No, no, no, sir. The Fight Club is in no way connected to the intake process. It's just a game a few students are playing with one another. While it is dangerous, it isn't illegal, so long as they're not collecting money to do it. I think they got the idea from watching 'Ultimate Fighter' on Spike TV."

"What about the paddle marks," Spears chimed in. "I suppose that you're going to tell me that they got those when they fell on their butts wrestling each other?"

"No...The three guys you took pictures of, illegally, say that those paddle marks were inflicted on them by each other. They say that they wanted to toughen themselves up for the Fight Club, so they thought paddling would build up their endurance to pain."

"That's just masochistic," said Spears. "But not illegal," I added.

"It's not going to be tolerated on this campus Chance," said President Johnson.

"I know Sir. Fortunately, none of these Fight Club events took place on campus, so the school isn't liable for any damages. I warned the students that the institution would not tolerate violent behavior, even wrestling, and advised them to cease all Fight Club activities. As far as I know they've complied."

"They had better comply!" President Johnson bullied. "I've heard about all I can stand from you and Spears, Chance. I see that nothing is going to become of this meeting. I am going to adjourn for the day and discuss this case with Dr. Jackson. My secretary Margaret will contact you both with my decision on this matter. Mr. Bradshaw, do you have anything to say about this on the fraternity's behalf?"

It was clear that in all his 32 years in the fraternity, Raymond Bradshaw had never heard anything like what he was hearing right now. Grabbing at his collar to unloosen the tie that made his collar dig into the rolls of his neck fat, he said wearily, "I-I- I don't know what to say about this, Brothers. We are Brothers, and we should behave towards one another accordingly. I'm not sure who's to blame for what, or whom did what to whom. All I know, is that this situation is ugly, with a capital "UG," it behooves us all to table this matter, and keep it within the confines of this room, until we get this whole mess sorted out." We all agreed silently.

That was fine by me. As I said earlier, reporting hazing does no one involved any good. The "victims" don't get into the frat, and if they do make it in, they are blackballed on the streets before the ink dries on their name on the roster. The so-called "perpetrators" are expelled from school, put in jail, and levied heavy civil fines that it is impossible for them to pay. Limestone College, least of all, could afford the bad publicity and lawsuits that a hazing case would surely bring. I'm sure Bradshaw wouldn't have been too happy to report to his superiors that a lawsuit was brewing in his territory either. No one at an HBCU like Limestone wants to see another Black

Man go to jail or drop out of school. I knew going into the President's office that as long as my story could put the situation at a stalemate, Spears' hazing report would not escalate into a full-blown hazing case. Needless to say, the 2004 Lambda Gamma line went over on time, as scheduled, April 13th, 2004, the day after the Mardi Gras Ball. But they didn't get to have a coming out show. The school put a moratorium on coming out shows on campus, because they didn't want the Bruz receiving any more publicity that semester than they already had gotten. The chapter was also barred from participating in intake for two semesters after that.

Spears kept his job, but I was suspended from work for a year. Ostensibly, it was for not reporting the Fight Club sooner, but in reality, it was for arguing administration into a stalemate. No one in that room believed my Fight Club story but arguing against it was futile because the only evidence to refute my defense was Spears spurious pictures and letter. No one ever brought up the incident again in public, and no one knows what happened to those pictures. But we still joke about Spears at the plot. Raymond Bradshaw even calls Spears "Seymour Hynee" behind his back to this day.

THE NEOS

L ambda Gamma's pledge process is not designed to hurt anyone; it is designed to prepare aspirants for life as a fraternity member, after they get off line. Life in the frat is lived, not only on campus, at parties, or at community service events, it is also lived every day, out in the real world. This is a frat lesson I learned over time, but the crux of its message is usually never gleaned by neophyte members as soon as they get off line. Once a new Bruh goes over, he's transported into an entirely new world of associations, language, and in-group signs. But his old world still exists, and probably reminds him of its existence every day. A lot of Neos, and Bruz in general, OD on the frat world because it has the power to be so absorbing. But, like Spears and myself, getting too swept up in fraternal zeal can have detrimental consequences to your non-fraternal life. I try to teach this lesson to every line I come into contact with. Some listen, most don't. But they all eventually learn it, and learn to deal with it, one way or the other.

The '04 line was not only the last LG line I pledged personally, it was also the last line I road tripped with. For some reason, I felt it a final duty to them, to show the '04 Bruz what frat life was like outside of Limestone College. Since I had free time, I had nothing to lose, really. Me, Dirty Red, Daryll Rivers and a few other older Bruz took the Neo's down to Walton University in South Carolina, after they went over, to see the 2004 Bruz at that school have their coming out show. For those who have never been to a coming out show, this may be a hard scene to conceptualize.

It was a rainy Friday night, so all the night's festivities would take place indoors. The actual coming out show was going to be held on campus in the gymnasium. But before that began, the Bruz where hosting a pre-party at the frat house. We arrived fashionably late, of course, so we only caught the tail end of the festivities which consisted of three kegs, 30 boxes of Bojangles chicken, assorted fixins, and a myriad of Bruz, women, and miscellaneous hangers-on. Luckily, we arrived in time to catch the pre-party before it shut down. I was barely into my meet-and-greet mode when the house manager kicked everyone out so that we could make our way over to campus to watch the show. I pocketed three cans of beer for the road and some chicken before we left.

When we got to the gymnasium, it smelled like a gymnasium, but it was packed to capacity with Black people of every shape, size and color. Most were Greek and wearing any and all type of wildly assorted paraphernalia. The place looked like a carnival stuffed into a college basketball court with bleachers pushed back. The Bruz set the place up so that guests could party before and after the coming out show. After that was over, any visiting Bruz who wanted to stay the night at Walton could go back to the frat house and party the night away or crash until their ride was ready to go home.

Things were in full-swing when the DJ cut off the music to announce the arrival of the night's featured guests: "The Brave

Hearts." The '04 line of the "Battling" Beta Sigma Chapter was comprised of seven men, thoroughly immersed in the TRUE Bruz spirit. I'd never seen them before in my life, until they marched out onto that stage. I knew they were good Bruz because Beta Sigma was one of those traditional chapters that held on to the old ways despite being immersed in an all-white campus. Their Neophytes were Big, Bald, Black, in fatigues, and wearing hockey masks. They reminded me of me and my line during our Hell Night. They were together, unified, Brothers on a similar mission, in a similar struggle. As a symbol alone, to the audience, they were nothing less than an awe inspiring creation of God. When they marched in, the lights were out, and all you could hear in the gym was what sounded like a hundred hoof beats pounding their way toward the stage from in back of the curtains.

The crowds' collective heart paused for a full measured breath when the lights came on, and "The Brave Hearts" stood there, triumphantly. I was about twenty feet away from the stage, with my right arm stretched out vertically, acting as a tripod for my video camera. There were a few faint "Make 'em wait Bruz!!!" shouted here and there in the gym, but overall, it was quiet because no one wanted to miss a word of what was about to be said. The Dean of the line, Montell "Loco" Montgomery, who also acted as the stage General in this particular production, looked like Fidel Castro himself in his battle gear. His voice reigned over the spell-bound audience as he introduced "his Boys" to the world. At the top of his lungs, he hollered to the furthest person in the back of the room: "It is my distinct, honor, and pleasure, to bring to you, the 2004 line of the Battling Beta Sigma Chapter, The Brave Hearts." The crowd went hysterical with cheer. Instantly, the entire line gave a fierce, long growl, stamping their feet in unison, to signify that they were ready to perform. The crowd went giddy with voiced anticipation for an enthusiastic performance. Loco let the display ride for a few seconds, but then harshly yelled "tighten up," and the Neos jumped into place military style to prove their discipline. For the next thirty minutes, the Neo's on stage were the stars of the organization, reciting poems and greetings that they learned while on line; performing traditional "steps" different old heads taught them, and acting out funny skits that they used to keep the heat off of them when they were in the hole. Dirty Red turned to me at one point in the show and said: "My shirt, these brands, they don't mean shit tonight, them niggaz on stage is the superstars here tonight." I passed him one of the beers in my pocket. I didn't have time to pay attention to Red, the Neo's were performing my favorite song, "Zoom." The Ace, called the step, with a surprisingly strong bass voice for a man of only 5'6". His line joined in with him for the adlibs.

Somebody tell me why…(Zoom, Zoom, Zoom…) Why
are we treated so Bad?…(Zoom, Zoom, Zoom…)
Oh…I wanna know, I need to, I gotta know… Why
are we treated so bad…(Zoom, Zoom, Zoom…)
I go to sleep at 6…(Zoom, Zoom, Zoom…) And
wake up early at 8…(Zoom, Zoom, Zoom…)
I go to see my Big Brothers, Big Brothers,
Big Brothers, Big Brothers …
But I'm always late…(Zoom, Zoom, Zoom…)
Oh…I wanna know, I need to, I gotta know… Why
are we treated so bad?…(Zoom, Zoom, Zoom…)
I got ache in bones…(Zoom, Zoom, Zoom…) And I
just want to go home…(Zoom, Zoom, Zoom…)

I just wanna see my Sweet Lady, Pretty
Lady, Pretty Baby, Pretty Lady …
Because I'm so all alone…(Zoom, Zoom, Zoom…)
Oh…I wanna know, I need to, I gotta know… Why
are we treated so bad?…(Zoom, Zoom, Zoom…)

About midway through the show, Preston "Marsh" Anderson, the number seven on the '04 LG line, taps me on the shoulder and tells me that he has a problem. "What is it Preston, I'm taping," I said.

"Sorry, Sir, but it's just…" I cut him off.

"Quit calling me Sir damn it! You're not on line anymore. It's Fierce, or Chance. What's up?"

"Yes, Sir – I mean Fierce. It's just that, there is this big ass Bruh over there who says I should know who he is. I don't, and now he's acting all belligerent about me not knowing."

"So?"

"So – what do I do to get him away from me?" Neophyte confusion, its normal.

"First of all, why would you want him to get away from you? You two are in the same organization, aren't you?"

"Yeah"

"Which just so happens to be dedicated to unity, right?"

"Yeah"

"Well, doesn't it make more sense to try to get to know this strange man whom you would have no other reason for possibly affiliating with, if it weren't for the fact that you two are in the same fraternity?" He'd never thought of the possibility.

"Oh, Yeah!!!"

"He's asking you a question, discreetly, to see whether you're real, or fake? Go talk to him, you might make a friend." I love talking in riddles to Preston, he really gets what I'm getting at, even when he doesn't get what I'm talking about.

"What do you mean? He sent me over here to get you after I told him I came with you."

"Really? Why didn't you say so?" I didn't know the guy Preston was talking about, or why he sent Preston over to get me. But I went anyways to show Preston that Black men need to overcome their fear of one another. If we are going to live together in unity, somebody has to be brave enough to extend the olive branch. Preston was a 270-pound mama's boy, who was unequivocally going to grow-up to be a middle-management paper pusher. The Bruh he was talking about was more than likely acting hostile toward Preston to intimidate him, but Preston backing down to the man's aggression (within the context of frat) shows a suspect demeanor that deserves to be interrogated.

The Bruh in question was named Damon "Franchise" Bowler. He was the number ten, on the Fall '02, Phi Omega line, from Constance College in Columbia, SC. He told me he was charging Preston up because the number ten on Preston's line, James "Franchise" Charles, wasn't there with us that night. He had a spring ball game that night. "How your LB gonna miss his first road trip, and you let him?" He grilled

Preston. "Y'all is supposed to roll together as one, ain't ya? You don't get this time back, you ain't gonna be in undergrad forever." I couldn't disagree with his logic. "Y'all is acting like you didn't pledge or something." Here it comes.

By this time most of Preston's LB's who did make it where gathered around us. Some were genuinely interested in what was going on, others were huddled around because we were the only faces that they recognized in a sea of Greeks. Franchise decided to make his point, the hard way. "Come on big boy, you and me gonna wreck!" Preston was dumbfounded. He looked to me to save him, but I just shrugged my shoulders, leaving it up to him to decide what to do next.

The look of determination in Franchise's eyes let me know that he was clearly the dictator of this situation. "I'm going to wreck you because your tail ain't here. Then I'm going to wreck all of your LB's who came with you, because none of you know anything about the frat." I had to keep myself from busting a gut. I'd seen this scene too many times before.

Carlos asked me if I was going to stop it, I shook my head and said, "Nope!" Preston Anderson was a marshmallow masquerading as college-aged man. I let this altercation ride because I saw where it was going, and decided P-Diddy needed to grow some hair on his chest. As he walked outside toward the back of the gymnasium, I could see that it finally dawned on him that this "Franchise" guy was serious, and got his stats up by wrecking easy-target Bruz like himself. To his credit, P gave Franchise all the fight that he had in him, which lasted about 10 seconds. Preston's feet spent about 8.5 of those seconds, elevated in the air, above his head and body, right before Franchise suplexed him. Fortunately, it was springtime so the grass cushioned his fall.

Frat rules say that wrecking is supposed to be the best two out of three, but by his fifth match, Franchise had pretty much wrecked the entire '04 LG line. The Ace, Justin dislocated his shoulder after his second wreck, and Carlos forfeited both his turns, and Preston was too tired after his first slam to venture a second try. Dirty Red was hot, because he couldn't stand for the chapter to lose face to anyone. I could tell that his next move was going to be taking his shirt off and giving the Franchise a go for his money.

"Man, you niggaz couldn't wreck a broken car, if you was drivin' drunk!" He yelled at the Neo's exasperatedly. "Where the hell is y'all's Honcho?" With that Preston went to go find Vincent "Trife" Tucker, his Honcho.

The Honcho is the person on line who can take the brunt of the physical punishment while on line. The Honcho is also usually the most wrecking Bruh on the line as well. Every Bruh is not expected to be a football player, but it always pays to have at least one muscle- bound giant on the line, just in case a situation calls for brawn over brains. Trife was from South Carolina, and he had been attending Bruz parties since his senior year in high school. Of all his line brothers, he was the only one naturally at ease in the Bruh environment. The only disturbance to his rhythm that he experienced that night was Preston getting him to go wreck with Franchise.

Trife was an all-American cruiser weight wrestler and football player taking up military studies at Limestone. Hand-to-hand combat was right up his alley. I had to explain to him that wrecking wasn't personal, and that it wasn't a fight, so he couldn't throw any punches. He sucked his teeth at me, as if I foiled his plan, but he was still enthused about the whole affair. He sized up pretty well to Franchise only losing three inches to him in height, and matching up almost perfectly to him in terms of weight.

When they locked up, it looked like a Spartan movie. The easy time franchise had with Preston and the others was a distant memory as Trife met Franchise chest to chest for the first six seconds of their grapple. After much struggle, and a quick hip toss, Trife slammed Franchise to the ground – HARD! Franchise got up, dusted himself off, and mumbled something under his breath about how he slipped.

"Nigga you didn't slip, yo' ass got handled!" Dirty Red screamed. He had to relish in the moment, because he might not get another chance to. Franchise just scowled at him for a split second, and then re-focused his energy on Trife.

"One more time Big Man," he said to Trife, and the two locked up on more time like pit bulls. Once again, Trife got the better footing and hold on Franchise. This time, however, there would be no question as to whether or not it was a legitimate win or not, Franchise's feet were clearly off the ground, along with most of the rest of his body too. He conceded his loss before his back hit the ground. When he got up, he shook Trife's hand, and went to get him a beer. That night we all stayed at the frat house and Franchise taught Preston and his LB's some fraternity chants that even I had never heard before.

Dirty Red is known for a lot of things, but his sparkling sense of humor is not one of them. I do believe, however, he cracked a smile to mask the tear he was about to shed when he saw the '04 LG Bruz fellowshipping with their sands.

THE FRAT HOUSE

Despite my now cavalier attitude toward my suspension from Limestone, at the time I was anything but calm when I got the news of my forced departure. Although I was quietly dignified about my departure, I was horrified on the inside. What would I do, and how would I survive? I only had a bachelor's degree at the time and was still taking masters classes that my job in the library was paying for. Not to mention that I lived in an apartment furnished by the school and had monthly child support payments to contend with. Fortunately, I am the Bruz, and part of what we're trained to do is survive through rough circumstances. Also fortunate for me was the fact that most of the Bruz have no problem acting as a support system for one another.

When I came into work that Monday following the hazing meeting, I was greeted by another white envelope sitting on my desk. I d idn't like the way the letter felt in my hands when I picked it up. It was too heavy. If good news were concealed inside the envelope it would only have been the size of a sheet of paper. This envelope had to contain at least three sheets folded. Those extra sheets weren't concert tickets, so I knew I wasn't out of the woods yet.

Once I mustered up the courage to open it, the letter inside said that "regrettably" the President's investigative committee (him & Jackson) found that my negligence as a college administrator inadvertently placed Limestone College's student population in unnecessary danger. "Although it is the University's belief that you, Mr. Chance, are an asset to Limestone College's community of scholars, our employee handbook clearly states that 'No college administrator shall be deemed negligent in their duty to maintain the safety of Limestone's student population in any manner.' The University does not hold you personally responsible for any criminal mischief or damages but fail-safes have been placed in the system for instances such as these, and protocol must be maintained." The letter contained a pink slip, and an eviction letter attached to instructions for vacating my office and apartment by weeks end. Dr. Johnson even ended the letter with a sardonic "You have a bright future ahead of you Mr. Chance, I hope that you consider re- applying with Limestone College again in the future."

Crisis situations, call for crisis thinking. Unfortunately, I was all out of good ideas. I was as hurt as I was dumbfounded at the verdict. I could go appeal the decision with Human Resources, or even President Johnson himself, but that would only make the situation worse. I knew that suspending me was Johnson's way of setting an example and signaling to anyone who might be watching that his fraternal ties did not overshadow his loyalty to the school and his own position. Me and my big mouth, telling them about the Fight Club; but I had to do it to save everyone else who could have been implicated had I not decided to concoct a palatable version of the story. Bruz got jobs and families. Shit, I did too. At least no one inquired about anyone else's involvement other than me, the undergrads and the pledges. My guess is that we were the only ones the school had jurisdiction over, so they decided to keep it in-house. Bradshaw backed away because none of the allegations were substantiated by the pledges. To him, the whole case was a matter of Bruz arguing with each other using the system. He'd met Spears before and knew what a tight ass he could be. None of the undergrads got suspended.

I needed to think so I left my office, after packing everything in it I valued, and went to my fortress of solitude: the plot. It was 9:30am, on a Monday, so the campus was active. But everyone seemed to be moving in slow motion to me. They were walking by, headed toward their respective destinations, but they weren't going anywhere. They were stuck and stiff. Plato's cave dwellers. They were all preparing themselves to be compartmentalized. They all needed to pledge. Take a set of wood and loosen up.

How could I be suspended? I was the good guy. I was carrying on tradition. The people punishing me knew it. They were Bruz. But still they felt it necessary to penalize me for doing the Bruz work. I felt betrayed. But blaming others for my actions does no good, so I got on the phone and called the one Bruh I knew I could count on in a time of extreme need.

Kenneth "Wreck-a-sorus" Simmons was a gentle giant. At 6'5", 265 lbs, I don't think Ken ever wrecked anybody. He was just too nice. He pledged at Alabama State in 1992. He lives in Charlotte now and is a computer network design consultant that spends a good bulk of his free time trying to see how fast a Coors silver bullet can shoot him in the face. The best Bruh you'd ever want to meet though. He would always say to, "If I say I'm gonna do something for you, you're gonna find me doing it, or on my way to do it." I knew that Ken dabbled in real estate pretty heavily and had rental property in Salisbury. Hopefully he wouldn't mind sacrificing an empty space for an unemployed friend with only one more steady paycheck coming his way until he found a new job. He picked up the phone on the second ring.

"Ken Simmons"

"What Up, Fierce Dawg!!!" he yelled into the receiver. Ken was always extra excited about everything.

"Brotha I need your assistance," I said in my most somber voice. Ken liked when I feigned reverence when I talked. He said it made me sound like I should be a preacher.

"Anything for you Fierce, I heard you got into a little trouble up there." Damn, how did he know?

"Nah, no trouble. Just life's circumstances, that's all." I had to keep showing the brave face. "But I do need a place to stay for a while."

"How long is a while?" "Until I find a job."

"Oh, one of those whiles…" I could hear him pondering over how to handle this situation in his head. "I think I might have something for you. One of the Bruz up there, Frank Higgins has a house he's been trying to get me to rent or buy. But it needs some work."

"I ain't fussy. I just need a place to cover my head until I get on my feet. Beggars can't be choosy." He laughed.

"Alright Dawg, I'll talk to him, and get back with you as soon as we work something out. But even if he doesn't want to do it, me and you can work something out. I ain't never gonna let the Bruz be out on the streets." I laughed. I was reassured. Ken always had a calming presence, even over the phone.

After I hung up with him, I called Mudd and told him that the undergrads would have to find a new advisor. I also told him to chill out on pledging the line because the heat was on. My next call was to Jeff Roberts because his wife worked at the unemployment office. Jeff picked up on the first Ring.

"Fierce, I already heard. I can't believe they fired you."

"I didn't get fired, I was suspended. I can come back after a year, if I want to." My dignity wouldn't let me accept what suspended meant.

"Did they suspend you from school too?" I hadn't thought about that.

"No. Apparently, I can give them money, but they won't pay me in return." I was blaming.

"How long do you have before you're done with your masters?"

"Another year after this one," how would I manage? "You'll make it. You're tough," Jeff was always a fountain of optimistic encouragement.

"Oh, I don't doubt it. But I do need a small favor from you."

"We don't do favors for each other Bruh, we just do."

"Good shit. I need to know what I have to do to get unemployment."

"That's easy, just make an appointment with my wife and file. Limestone won't fight your claim unless you quit." Jeff was so matter of fact about everything you'd think it was him who worked at Unemployment Office. "What else can I do for you?"

"Nothing, for now, but I appreciate the look out." "T'wernt nothing, Fierce. We all know what you did." Jeff was always cautious of his words over the phone because he was a State Trooper. "Hit me up if you need anything." We hung up.

My mid-morning strategy session was interrupted by Dr. Clarence Tumor, my supervisor from the library. Apparently, he got the news of my suspension before I did. He was watching me sit on the plot from his office window and came outside to see why I was milking the clock. A flame to his last name, he was switching as he walked up to me.

"Mr. Chance, I have heard about your unfortunate circumstances, but that is no excuse to dawdle on company time. I expect for you to have all of your affairs in order before you leave." I never understood why Tumor felt the need to adjust his bowtie every time he talked.

"Yes Sir," I said, even though I wanted to punch him in the face. Normally, I would make an excuse to justify my whereabouts, or at least say some slick shit to make it seem as if I was in the right, but I knew that if I was ever going to make it back into Limestone, I didn't need to burn anymore bridges than I already had. Tumor was looking for any excuse to make my suspension permanent, so I didn't need to give him any more ammunition. I returned to my office to finish cleaning it out, when Greg Kelly walked in.

"'Sup, Fierce. Why are you packing? Did you get fired?"

"No. Suspended." I kept my head down as I placed my books in a box, one-by-one.

"What? How the fuck could the school suspend you, nothing happened to anyone else, and they didn't find anything?"

"Because Limestone College is their festival, and I am the Paschal Lamb."

"What?" "Forget it"

Kells helped me finish packing and put my stuff in my car before lunch. Of all the neo's on the yard that year, Greg "Get'Er Done" Kelly was my right-hand man. If I was Shaq, he was Kobe (before all the arguing). At 5'2", Kells wasn't the most physically intimidating person you would want to meet, but in terms of heart, it would take a 6'10" linebacker to match the kind determination and loyalty Kells displayed on a regular basis.

"So, what are you going to do now?" he asked as we put the last boxes in the car.

"I don't know. I'm not really sure right now. But, something will give, it always does." I was still trying to keep up the brave face.

"You can stay in my dorm room with me if you don't have a place." Kells was too kind.

"Naw, I'm straight Dawg. I got a place lined up with Ken Simmons, but if that doesn't work out, I'll take you up on your offer." As we were talking, my lady lust, Ms. Tiffany Everhart, road by in her red Dodge Neon. She gave us a beep and wave, and I was stuck for a complete 5 seconds. She was a Delta, who worked in the president's office, and earned part-time money as the school's assistant volleyball coach. She played in college so she pretty much ran the team under the head coach, Andre Huff's direction.

"You got it bad for that young lady Fierce," Kells said. "I can tell by the way the two of you transfix on one another every time your paths cross."

"Is it that obvious?"

"The only question is why haven't you two bumped uglies yet?" He chuckled.

———◦∞∘•❀•∘∞◦———

Later on, that day, I got a call from Ken.

"Fierce Dawgy Dawg!!! What up?" Any mood of self-pity I was in was soon to be dissipated.

"What up Ken-O?"

"Did I tell you I was gonna come through for you?" He asked mockingly. "What did I say I was gonna do?"

I laughed as I spoke, "You said you were going to find me a place."

"And I am a Bruh of my word. Word is Bond!" I could hear him beating on his chest over the phone. "How good are you with a hammer?"

"I used to paint houses during the summer when I was in undergrad…"

"That's good enough." Ken butted in. "There will be plenty of painting to do after you finish demolishing the place."

"I'm not a messy tenant."

"I didn't say you were. You're going to be the project manager of my remodeling team."

"Remodeling Team?"

"Yes, remodeling team. I'm going to rehab Higgins' house and sell it for a profit."

"You bought it from him?"

"No. Not really. -Yet. I leveraged it from him by promising to remodel the joint for nothing more than the cost of materials."

"How are you going to do that?"

"By having my live-in labor do the work for me?" I could hear him smiling.

"Oh. I'm the labor." I abhorred manual labor. The reason I went to college was to get away from it. It's not that I can't swing a hammer. I took all the prerequisite shop classes in high school. But my life's vision wasn't geared toward being the hired help, and Ken knew it.

"I know what you're thinking, but look at it like this, all great artists have to sing for their supper some time in their lives. Your time is now." What a spin master.

"I'll think about it," which shouldn't take long.

"You don't have to. Meet me at the brown brick house around the corner from your apartment tomorrow at 5." He added for good measure, "What have you got to lose?"

He was right.

———∘∘⊰❂⊱∘∘———

Higgins' house was literally right around the corner from the two-bedroom flat I was renting from the school. 1001 Institute St. was a 3 bedroom, one story, brick ranch with a partially finished basement. My campus apartment on Monroe Street faced the school; Higgins' house was on the next immediate intersection, Institute, right at the corner facing Institute. The grass was a foot high, and the storm gutters were piled high with debris. There were bed sheets over the windows, and the back yard looked like salvage center. I knew that I was in for an experiment. The only thing new at the house was Ken Simmons' BMW parked conveniently underneath the carport. He jumped out of his seat as soon as he saw me hit the corner.

"Dawgy! Did I not tell you that I had your back?" His arms were outstretched wide. "You don't got to thank me; you just got to listen to my vision for this spot. Walk with me." He grabbed me by my shoulders and led me through the grand tour of his dream palace. When he unlocked the door, a spider web the size of a dinner plate stretched with the full expanse of the door's hinges. There were the remnants of lives lived strewn everywhere there was space in the house. Most of it was junk piled on top of junk, piled on top of junk. Ken could see the look of disgust in my face. "I forgot to tell you, Higgins is a bit of a pack rat."

"Dawg, you forgot to tell me Higgins was collecting dead bodies in here. What's that God awful smell in here?" Ken was trying to act as if he didn't notice it until I said something.

"Aw, that's just old musty air. Moth balls and stuff. Once you open some of these windows, you'll be fine. And with that,

Ken snatched one of the bed sheets off to reveal a flood of light. The exposed window also revealed that Higgins decided to bolt the windows to the house up around 1994. So, there was no way to let fresh air into the house.

"How long did Higgins say he owned this house?"

"I think since the 70's?" Ken loved making up facts he didn't know.

"And it's been boarded up how long?"

"It's not boarded up. This is a perfectly good house, if you have some vision." Ken was trying to sell me hard. Inevitably, he was only showing me an angle of his angle.

"You know what I meant."

"Look here Fierce this would be your room." He escorted me over piles of half open boxes and trash bags filled with memory's I'm sure Higgins would love to forget but was too scared to let go of. At the back of the house was the master bedroom. I could tell this room was the master suite because it had two closets. Typical for this type of 70's ranch bungalow.

"I can see the potential, but I really wasn't expecting to have to put this much labor into this project. It will take months to clean this place out, and maybe even years to get it up to code for regular living. Thank you. But, no thank you." I hated to seem ungrateful, but I wasn't a carpenter.

"Dawg, I haven't even told you the best part of the deal. Higgins is willing to let you stay here for free until the house is completely rehabbed." He got me again.

"Nothing's free Ken."

"It won't cost you your soul, just your smile." Damn Ken could sell sugar to a diabetic. "All you need is a roommate or two to help you with the renovations and bills, and you're good."

"Give me a night to think about it."

"Think, Schmink. Here are the keys. If you don't want it, give them back to me in the morning." He forced the keys into my hand as if they were a loan I didn't want to take. Although I was skeptical, it felt good to know that I had a place to go.

———◦◦◦❧◦◦◦———

Ironically enough, as I was looking for a place to stay, Mudd Ross was on the verge of creating a vacancy at his then current dwelling as well. Mudd was living with his LB, Rashad, and the both of them finally realized that friendship and roommates are not co-equal statuses. Rashad and Mudd were friends before they came into the frat, so it seemed natural that they share an apartment their junior year, once Rashad's sister Cookie moved out of their 2-bedroom apartment to live with her sorority sister, Carla. After one year of living with Rashad, Cookie decided that she only had one dad, and she'd left him in New Jersey, so it didn't make sense to be in college living with an older Brother who thought he was by some divine right an extension of their pops.

The only snag in this otherwise well thought out plan was that Mudd and Rashad were two totally different types of people. Sure, they had the frat in common, but after that, there was very little the two old chums could say they agreed about. Mudd was a Christian Pentecostal from South Carolina, and Rashad was Black Muslim from New Jersey. The two together were like the odd couple, but with more cussing. Mudd was a music and voice major, Rashad was an English and Political Science major. Mudd was rapper, Rashad was a youth counselor. When Mudd was working Rashad was asleep. When Rashad was working, Mudd was usually asleep. Every evening at about

10pm their worlds would collide for the two hours it took Mudd to wake up, and Rashad to wind down. This crucial two hours was the source of their problem because during that interval all the two could manage to do was bicker about who was doing whom wrong. Rashad thought that Mudd was rude, crude, and loud. Mudd looked at Rashad as an uptight snob, who needed to learn to have some fun in life.

Things hit a boiling point with the two when Cookie had to spend the week back at her big brother's place because Carla had several family members in town that week visiting, and her boyfriend was on a road trip with the track team. Cookie was perfectly okay with sleeping on the couch, since Mudd took over her room, but it was Rashad who became uncomfortable with his sister's visit when he came home from work one night and noticed that Cookie had found her way back to her old room.

Mudd's only excuse for the affair was "we both grown, so what's the problem?" Cookie had nothing to say to anyone about anything. She just didn't want her boyfriend to find out. Apparently, Cookie had never thought Mudd that attractive because he was clearly not the settle down and get married type. But, according to her, there was something uniquely sensual about being alone with Mudd. She found this out on her second day of staying with the roommates. She was getting out of the shower preparing to go to bed, and Mudd was just waking up to start his nightly rounds. Half groggy, he stumbled into the steamy bathroom to relieve himself, not remembering that they had a house guest. Cookie had just stepped out of the shower so the water was not running loud enough to warn Mudd that someone was in the rest room. Cookie was so startled to see a fully stiff Mudd with no shirt on standing in the doorway in front of her that she dropped her towel to cover up her mouth as she screamed. In the split second it took for the two to finally recognize who it was that they were looking at, both realized that they'd never really seen the person in front of them before.

Two days after this initial encounter, Rashad got off of work thirty minutes early. When he got to the house, he was bewildered by the darkness of his apartment. At first, he thought nothing of it, and flicked on the living room lights. Curiously, Cookie wasn't there on the couch like normal, but he dismissed her absence as unimportant. On his way to the kitchen to fix one last snack before hitting his books, he noticed that there were voices coming from Mudd's room. Devilishly excited, he snuck over to Mudd's room to hear what the voices were saying. If he was lucky, he could catch Mudd in the throws of passion with one of his hoochie lady friends. A woman's voice, sure enough, was what Rashad heard through the door. Mudd was giving her the business too. She kept screaming his name at the top of her lungs. "Mudd, Mudd, Mudd!!!" Rashad was doubled over laughing to himself in hysterics until Mudd opened the door, and Cookie walked out wearing one of Mudd's t-shirts. It took Rashad a month to talk to either one of them after that night.

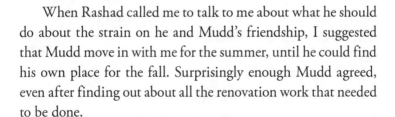

When Rashad called me to talk to me about what he should do about the strain on he and Mudd's friendship, I suggested that Mudd move in with me for the summer, until he could find his own place for the fall. Surprisingly enough Mudd agreed, even after finding out about all the renovation work that needed to be done.

"Can I play my music anytime I want to?" was his only real question to me after he found out he'd be living rent free for a while.

"I don't give a shit what you play or when you play, as long as you're down for the get down when it comes to the rehab," was my very relieved response. Mudd came from a family of South Carolina lumberjacks so working with his hands was second nature. Although he definitely considered himself an artist, more so than a laborer, Mudd had done his fair share of carpentering before he left the woods. It seemed that even though I had fallen, all the pieces were coming together to make a pretty soft landing for me after all.

We got two bedrooms habitable on the main floor of the house in about a day. It was no easy task, but Mudd and I hauled 76 boxes and two water beds out of those two rooms. We placed them in the living room on top of all the other boxes of crap that furnished the house. We pulled up the carpet in each room because the stench of the mildew was keeping an unhealthy bacteria in the air.

The house ran north to South, with its front face facing east. Our bedrooms were on the southwestern side of the house. The living room was on the northeastern side of the house. And the kitchen was behind it, on the southwestern side of the house. To the south of the kitchen was a wooden den that looked like Higgins used it as a mini library. To the south of it, was a small bedroom with its own mini bathroom, complete with a tiled stand-up shower.

"Man, Higgins used this room as his personal fuck spot," Mudd joked as we were excavating boxes from room.

In reality, Higgins was a bachelor after his first wife died, so he might have been a player. But with three kids to raise by himself, I doubt it. But whatever Higgins was doing in that house before he moved, it was something he didn't want everyone knowing about. No normal person would have kept all of these memories so tightly locked away who didn't want to forget them. I was just happy that I wouldn't be sleeping underneath a bridge.

We took possession of the Higgins House two weeks before the 04 line was supposed to go over. It was also three weeks after the chapter's underground pledge process was stopped by Nationals halt of the official process. We never resumed the underground process after the official process restarted because no one was sure what the complete fall out of the case would be. Everyone quietly left the decision to go or not go up to me because I was the DP, and most immediate past advisor. I didn't say a word about starting again because I was more concerned with my living situation than anything, plus, Darryl was the acting advisor, so I figured he'd pick up the torch. I figured wrong, but Rivers set me straight the morning he came over to the new place to "check up on me."

"What's up Fierce? How's the house coming?" He said when I opened the door and motioned for him to come in. "Bruz have been worried about you, no one has seen or heard from you in about a week."

"Why worry, I got me."

"Well, everyone is also worried about the line, and when you're gonna start those guys up again. The National deadline is coming up soon. I told everyone you're gonna hold a set here tonight."

"Hold up, what set? Where? And who the hell is everybody."

"Here. Higgins said it was okay, and I told the potentials to meet up here at 9. Don't worry though; I instructed them all to leave campus on foot alone. When they get…"

"Hell No!"

"Awe, don't be like that Fierce. The Bruz need you. Tonight is the 13th anniversary reunion for Dirty Red's line. There were thirteen of them on line, so I told him and his LB's that they could come to see the boys tonight."

"What the fuck are you talking about? Those boys are through as far as I'm concerned. Teach 'em some hops, give them the test, and read 'em in!"

"Dog, you know them dudes ain't finished, and they haven't been touched in a month. We might have to extend their process beyond the school's deadline."

"Oh no, I'm not pledging any Bruh after he's already a Bruh. That just seems sacrilegious." I was serious. "Once a man is over, you're no longer teaching him to be a man, you're teaching him to let you get your rocks off."

Well, you better teach them something quick because the 90's Bruz said they will be here line deep at 11 o'clock."

"Man, fuck them and fuck you! Do one of you have a job for me?"

I told the potentials to meet me at the house at 5pm that day for two reasons. One, I wanted to make sure that the campus had died down a bit before I called them over. And, two, I needed their help to begin cleaning out the basement of the Higgins house. Mudd and I began unearthing some of the ruins contained in that dungeon, but by 4 o'clock we'd barely scratched the surface. I suggested we come up for air and wait on reinforcements. So, we sat on the back patio, drinking Gatorade, and talking until the potentials arrived.

"This place has got a lot of potential, Fierce. Did you see that there is another waterbed downstairs, and a fireplace?"

"Yep. Higgy Hig was doin' it big in the 80's." I joked. "What does he do anyways?" I forgot Mudd had never even been formerly introduced to Higgins.

"He's the superintendent of schools. Back then, he was just a teacher though." Higgins was also the ace on the '02 grad line, he was 52 years old, so we named him "Methuselah." When he met new Bruz, he would always tell them, "I'm old as dirt, ugly as sin, but I still get mo pussy then most men," and end his greeting with a huge belly laugh that showed off the diamond inside his gold front tooth. He was genuinely a good egg but remained conservative in his public life because of his social and professional stature. His deal with Ken was the perfect way for him to help out a brother in distress, without harming himself in the process. He agreed to let me stay there because he knew that if I turned out to be a bad tenant the responsibility for my actions, short of destruction to the house, fall back on Ken's shoulders because he holds the primary lease on the property. I was a sub-lessor. I respected that, so I was uneasy about letting the Bruz come and run over the property. Even though I lived there, I knew from my real estate courses that Frank Higgins was the only person who owned a security interest in the place. I wasn't going to let his place be run down or scandalized by the illicit activities of a few Bruz. But I couldn't deny that by living at that house, with its immediate proximity to the campus, I was willfully placing myself at the epicenter of all things Bruh related on campus. And I did decide to use my position to my advantage.

When the potentials arrived, I immediately put them on box patrol. They formed a human assembly line that hoisted boxes from the basement to back porch. Higgins and his family were supposed to come by when we were finished to sort through the boxes and decide what he wanted to do with it.

Surprisingly, all ten of them showed up, staggering in two by two. I hadn't spoken with them all as a group since the night we got the letter from Nationals, but they were all still hungry and eager to continue their journey through the Fight Club. Things being what they were, however, I was still a bit hesitant as to how to proceed from here. Who had they been talking to since our last meeting? I knew that they knew that Nationals had stepped in. I also knew that they knew that they were pretty much a shoe in to get into the frat, so really there was no need to continue pledging. The weed-out process was over. But yet, they were still there, hauling and toting, shoulder-to-shoulder, with me and Mudd as if they had just as much of a personal interest in reviving old Higgins' House as we did. And then it hit me – they did! Or at least they should.

"You know what," I said during a group water break. "It's a shame this old house has been sitting here all this time rotting away doing nothing for years. Higgins or the school should be doing something with it, student housing or something." Everyone who was listening was nodding their head in agreement. And then Carlos interjected.

"Why doesn't the school have fraternity and sorority houses like other schools?"

"That's a good question." I said. "I read in the fraternity history book that Limestone College did have a fraternity house at one point in time, but when I tried to look up more information on it in the school's library, there wasn't even a mention of it in the year books." My wheels were turning. "But, then again, who needs history, when every day is a chance to make a little bit of it on your own?" Mudd started smiling because he loved my philosophical quotes. "The only thing stopping us from making this into our frat house, is our own ambition." A few of those present gave an enthusiastic "YEAH!!!" in unison.

"But won't we have to get the school's permission, Fierce?" Preston asked.

"Aw, quit being a pussy, Preston," Carlos said. "They'll most likely be mad, but that's their problem," I replied. "This is a private residence, so the best that they could do is complain that they've got a nuisance neighbor."

"You think Higgins will agree to it?" Mudd asked. "He's the Bruz, of course he will," I wasn't really sure. "Besides, Ken Simmons owns the lease interest in this house, and as long as there is nothing in his contract that says he can't turn this place into a frat house, there is nothing stopping us from doing it."

Ironically enough, Ken pulled up at precisely that moment. His car looked as if it was stuffed with rations to feed an Army. "What up Fierce Dawg!!!" he said with his head hanging out of the drivers-side window as he pulled up. He got out the car, poking his chest out as if he'd just conquered the world single-handedly.

"What's all this shit in the car?" I asked out of genuine curiosity, as well as hunger.

"This, my friend, is a teaching moment." He was grinning from ear-to-ear like a man trying to sell me something. He'd been doing that non-stop since he first showed me this place. "I've been thinking Fierce, what is Limestone College missing that most other colleges have? A frat house." Great minds think alike. "All we need to do is get those new guys on board, and we could change the culture of this whole town." Ken was always grandiose. "I figure that since I'm going to be renting this house out to some college student's anyways, why not rent it to the Bruz. At least I know who I'm renting it to." "Well, they're all in the back yard, clearing out the basement, so ask 'em." I laughed as I talked. We walked to the backyard.

"Alright, who knows how to work a grill?" Ken asked. Ivan and Shawn, the #6 raised their hands. "Well, I want you two to go to my car, take out that grill, bring it back here, and get it fired up. You..." He was snapping his fingers, pointing, trying to remember Preston's real name, finally he gave up, "Fat boy, you and the Mexican go get that food out of the car, and put it in the refrigerator, so those two can start cooking. Makes no sense for everybody to be out here working with no food, right? The rest of you huddle up around me for a second." The potentials formed a semi-circle around me and Ken.

"I'm not going to bullshit y'all. You guys are most likely going to get into the frat. But that don't mean shit, unless you make it mean some shit. Right now, you've got a black stain over you because of how fucked up your process has been. But once you go over, no one will be able to hold that against you, unless you let them hold it against you. The best way to make them forget is by putting in work for the frat. I know some of you live on the yard, and some of you stay off campus, but this house here is where y'all should consider making your campus home. Together, we could make sure that Bruz who come in through Lambda Gamma always have a place to stay."

And with that speech, the Bruz frat house in Salisbury was born (again). That night Dirty Red and three of his seven LB's who actually made it into town showed up to meet the '04 Bruz. The taxing that we put on them at the hole was nothing compared to what they went through in the basement of the frat house. Thunderation, the # 8 off of the 1990 line, was a two-time all-CIAA Limestone College baseball star, and now he's a physical therapist in Tampa, FL. He attributes his tremendous swing to knowing exactly where to pinpoint a man's crumple zones. According to him, "Each man is built different, but the human body is just the same in us all in general. If I can make that lesson reverberate through this here stick of lumber, I can make that lesson reverberate through those men's lives."

During one set, he folded the honcho and tail three times a piece, on his first swing. "And I'm just getting warmed up Boys!!!" is all he kept saying all night. The '90 Bruz knew that this was the last night that the older members of the chapter were going to get a chance to pledge this line, so they went extra hard on the '04 boys. In a very makeshift manner, this night in the frat house was the 2004 Bruz hell night. My pride in their endurance is part of the reason I agreed to take them on the road trip after they went over.

The 90's Bruz were mercilessly wild, a true reflection of their times. Jonathan "Mac Nasty" Carter, the number one on the 1990 line, even burnt the history test in front of Ivan and told him to recite the answers to everything contained in the test to him before it finished burning. The punishment for not being able to do so was a disintegrated study guide, and four stokes of wood from Thunderation. They kept them boys going until three in the morning. It wasn't all beating though. The Neos learned chants, and steps, and the protocol of the chapter. They heard real life stories about the men who came through Lambda Gamma Chapter before them, and the benchmark of excellence that they had set within the Limestone College community. Dirty Red said to them, "Everything around here ain't roses and sunshine. But, for damn sure, we're the ones that tend the garden and tell everyone what the weather's gonna be like." That was his way of saying the Bruz rule.

Thunderation said, "I'm going to give all of you, my card. Call me when you go over. Anything you, or the chapter needs, if I can provide it for you, I will." He had a sobering amount of pride in his eyes when he left them. I was sure I would see him at Mardi Gras next month.

THE LOAFERS

The only neophyte from the '04 line to move into the frat house, and stay, was Carlos. That summer, Mudd and I, with the help of just about every Bruh in Rowan County, grad and undergrad, on some level, completely removed all remnants of the Higgins era in the house. We painted, and even found out that there was an electric exhaust vent hooked up to the main floor hall designed to suck all of the noxious air out of the house. For good measure, Mudd and I removed all of the bolts off of the storm windows so that house could breathe and detoxify itself. After two months of stalling, Higgins claimed all of his old boxes and transferred them to his new house. Of the five boxes that Higgins did decide not to take, none of it looked any less valuable than the other junk he decided to hold onto so tightly. But what made the boxes that he didn't take with him so special, was that he placed them in a closet in the basement under lock and key. He made me and Mudd promise not to disturb them or the other contents of the closet. As strange of a request as it was, I let it go because after all, Higgins was doing us a huge favor.

Good old Ken Simmons was the unofficial sponsor of the Higgins House renovation project. Me and Mudd weren't really working anywhere full-time but at the house, so Ken paid all the bills except lights and water. I paid for the lights with money I earned from my part- time job working nightshift at a group home. And Mudd paid for the water with money he earned playing organ at Reverend Little's church. Ken also supplied us with a steady influx of food, smuggled from his wife's deep freezer. Ken didn't mind giving all his food away, that was just his personality. But he had to sneak us food because his wife, Rosie, learned early on in their relationship that she had to police Ken's altruism, or he would give them right into the poor house. Ken's motto that summer was "Keep the grill going!" And that summer, we kept the grill going day-in and day-out. Grilling was communal, and it broke up the boredom of rehabbing. Mudd tried to set a personal record for man hours logged in in-front of the smoke pit. He was pretty decent too, as long as I seasoned the meat. At any given hour of night, on any given day of the week, you could catch Mudd grilling underneath the carport. I was the house manager, I oversaw all the repairs and renovations, and made sure the lights and water were paid. I also made sure to keep up constant communications with all the Bruz young and old in the Salisbury area, because I wanted all of them to invest into the idea of maintaining a frat house when I left the property. It was easy keeping up with the Bruz at first because every Bruh in the city passed by the house daily as we were working, admiring our industry as if we were rebuilding the Great Pyramids. I remember Ralph Young, '83 LG, and now deputy sheriff of Rowan County, said "the place looks like a palace Bruz" when he saw the interior design of the two rooms me and Mudd had finished. Like us, he could see the possibilities of the blank tapestry that was the rest of the unfinished first floor. I didn't take him into the basement because we were still cleaning it out. For some insane reason, we all wanted space to be the Bruz. Modern life being what it is, we all secretly felt having a physical home for the Bruz in Salisbury would make the organization all that more real in our everyday lives; an actual force to be contended with. Even though I wasn't an employee of the school anymore, I still saw myself as, in some measure, responsible for the livelihood of the Bruz on campus. I was a 24/7 LG Bruh, and as a member of the chapter it was my duty to make sure that the Bruz survived on this campus. A frat house would keep the chapter alive and together forever.

When August came, and the students started to return to Limestone, Carlos called me and asked if it would be okay for him to stay with me and Mudd at the "frat house." Of course, I said "Sure!" If I would have had any common sense I would have said "heelll nooo" and this story would be cut short right, then and there. But, seeing as I didn't have the vision that I do now at that time, I let the name "frat house" linger in my mind (and the public eye) like a Broadway marquee. By accepting Carlos into the Higgins House, I implicitly accepted his whole line into the house, and they each used the "frat house" as their personal steppingstone into their emerging adult lives. I can chuckle at some of the things that happened in that house now, but back then, when it was going on, I remember being a tyrant about maintaining order in a house that was otherwise chaos. Although each one of them would grow to be an exemplary Black man in his own right, seeing all of the '04 line interact with one another at the frat house, showed me why Black men in American society are considered so dysfunctional. The rules of everyday living aren't set up for the inclusion of their lifestyle dynamics. In a young Black man's life there is always some drama; especially in his twenties. Whether it be external drama, or the self-imposed kind, most young Black men are going to have some type of beef going on in their lives. And moreover, most young Black men are going to beef out with other Black males about what they're beefing out about, rather than tending to the bigger picture that surrounds whatever it is that they're beefing out about in the first place. My theory was that the frat house could counter-act this penchant for conflict. I believed that a frat house would provide free space for Bruz of all backgrounds to meet on common ground and mentor one another about life, and hopefully mature the undergraduate Bruz faster and safer than any other alternative means. The frat house could also eliminate the need to pledge underground. Bruz from all generations needed a place to come home to as well. If I would have had my way, totally, the frat house would have been an elite command force's headquarters. But, since the frat is a popular consensus, my decision making had to move in the direction of the general body.

Carlos had to move into the frat house because he'd gotten kicked off of the yard the previous semester. The morning we came back from the South Carolina road trip, Carlos got a boot put on his car because he left it double parked behind the dorms overnight. Rather than follow normal protocol and pay the $90 fine to security to have it removed, Carlos went to his room, grabbed his tools, and removed the boot himself. No one bothered him about it for two days either, but when Chief Bromstead heard about someone circumventing his squad's authority, he reported Carlos to Dr. Jackson. Jakson in turned, penned a letter to Carlos, doubling his fine, and requiring him to pay the bill within one week or risk further unnamed disciplinary action. According to Carlos, he wasn't feeling rebellious, but he didn't pay the fine because he had no money. As a result of his delinquency, Dr. Jackson evicted Carlos from campus housing for the remainder of the 2004 calendar year. His misfortune was my luck, because with Carlos in the mix, I was sure that I would be able to continue to influence undergraduate affairs on campus.

When Carlos moved in, he moved in like a true college student moves in anywhere. He brought his whole life with him. It was compressed inside an overstuffed '92 Buick Regal. As he pulled up to the house, his car looked like his parents made him take everything that would fit in his car with him. As soon as he stepped out the car, Mudd greeted him with the grill spatula. Carlos didn't mind the work though, because it kept him around food, and away from manual labor. As we sat underneath the carport that first night, I laid out my plan for the school year to him, to see what it sounded like out loud. Mudd was there too.

"Bruz," I said. "I think that we should go full steam ahead this year trying to make this place into a frat house. It would be good for the Bruz and good for the school." Mudd and Carlos, shook their heads stoically agreeing as they passed a blunt between themselves. "No organization on this campus has a fraternity house, but I think that the concept would catch like wildfire if we pulled it off here for just a year." I shook my right index finger in the direction of the house to demonstrate my point.

"I'm wit it Fierce," Mudd mumbled as he exhaled smoke.

"Man, quiet as its kept Fierce, me and my LB's already had designs on this house since you guys first let us in here." Carlos said before he started laughing, "We knew what we were taking an ass whoopin' for. The frat ain't about the perks, but this house is definitely a perk."

And that it was. When everybody came back, the frat house became a switching station for the Bruz lives. We hung out there, we partied there, we crashed there, we held meetings there, and we had step practice together there. We had meals in the house, we had arguments in the house, and we had fights house. Boy, did we have arguments and fights in the house. But we were together. I used to always preach to the Neos, "This is only a moment in time. You guys are not going to be together forever. Cherish this time and experience that you have together. Once you graduate, the time you dudes spend together will be limited at best." Everyone used to shrug me off, but I was speaking wisdom. The Bruz just didn't understand how significant it was to have a cluster of leaders together during their most formative years. I also don't think very many Bruz in Salisbury, other than me, Mudd, Carlos, and Ken really understood the significance of having a place where ALL the Bruz could come and be themselves free of their social masks.

Carlos would always joke that I was a frat fanatic, but I was dead serious when I used to ramble on to him about the potential of the fraternity to act as an incubator for creating the type of leader Black America has said it yearns for. "Think about it Dawg," I said to Carlos one night as we were smoking underneath the carport. "You've got an organization of nothing, but college educated Black men who are striving to be leaders —

Whatever it is that the term 'leadership' refers to in this sense. And you've got them at one of the most vulnerable moments of their lives, the transition from boyhood to adulthood. Why not use a space like a frat house to intentionally train them to be the type of man that doesn't fall victim to the traps of American society. And moreover, why not teach them to teach other Blacks not to fall victim to the traps of American society. Keep in mind that when I say Blacks, I'm not talking about just African-Americans; or even every African-American necessarily.

When I say Blacks, I mean the poor and oppressed, who stand in opposition to the status quo of inequality."

"True. True. True." chimed in Brother Mudd, as if he were the deacon of First Shiloh Baptist. We thought he was asleep.

"All jokes aside, I'm dead serious. Think about it. Every Bruh who comes in as an undergrad is eventually going to weave himself so far into middle-class American society, that he is bound to be considered a community leader in some sense. So why not use the undergrad experience to give Black leaders a purpose?"

"I thought that pledging does give us a purpose?" Carlos interjected.

"Yes, it does, in a way. But it doesn't go far enough. Right now, the process – and I'm speaking strictly for the underground version because the above ground shit doesn't teach anything but how to pay money – it only teaches aspirants to struggle together through adversity, but it doesn't teach them how to struggle together (or individually for that fact) through prosperity. When the frat first started, I can see how important it was for Black men to learn to cope and excel amidst open adversity, but the dynamics of Black struggle has advanced beyond that paradigm solely.

Nowadays, Black men have just as much to fear by being successful as they do when they are nobodies. The lures of success can be just as, if not more deadly, than the trappings of poverty. We need to use this frat house as training ground for young educated Black men that trains them to utilize Limestone's resources as a gateway that will take them to the seat of U.S. power. It may sound like an idyllic dream, but I think that we have the collective means to be a decision-making factor in the way the world is run. All the dynamics are here. We've got doctor Bruz, lawyer Bruz, teacher Bruz, preacher Bruz, and just regular dude type Bruz too. What if all of them were marching to the beat of the same drum? Not just in rhetoric, but in actual lived mentality and action too?"

"You mean a concerted effort to push a 'Bruh agenda' on the world." Carlos laughed. I could see his theatrical mind imagining me dressed like Malcolm X, standing in front of an exaggerated globe giving my speech to the United Nations.

"Yes. Our shared value system magnified for public consumption. We're doing it already implicitly anyways. What do you think those history packets they give you guys are for, decoration? No, it's propaganda about the organization's tradition of leadership, and it's designed to inspire you guys to emulate those famous Black men you read about. Those men are all famous by public and fraternity standards. They supposedly exemplify what a Black leader looks like, and it is hoped that you gentleman follow their example and mold yourselves into what a Black leader should look like. I know it sounds too simplistic, but you've got to look the part, to get the part. Image is everything in this image-based society. So why not take the reins of your image, and turn this thing into the thing that the people really want to see? We've been stuck in the waiting for a messiah mode so long we forgot that the messiah was supposed to be a leader who ignited the leadership spark in each of us that we've always had. Tap into that spark that's inside you and the messiah is already here. I think that it is the frat house's duty to teach young Black men like you two, and the rest of the Neo's, to survive as the burden bearers of a tradition that sees us men of LG as the current leaders of Black people. I want y'all to take that role with you wherever you go and actualize it in whatever you do. Take ownership of your lives, make it yours."

"Man, the Bruz ain't gonna buy into that." Carlos mocked.

"Nah, I'm with you on that one Fierce," Mudd butted in. "Niggas need to start thinking on a deeper level, and what's thought if we don't put some action to it. I ain't perfect, but I do know that people are watching me, and I know that some of them be modeling their behavior after mine. Y'all know I cut the fool with the ladies, but I know what to say and how to act around them too. Most women got kids, or want to have some, so they make little mental notes on how you behave in public to judge how you would act around their kids. I learned that from my Auntie." Now I bust into hysterics.

"Leave it to good old Mudd to turn my high-minded philosophy into simple pragmatism." I was the only one who thought that that last one was funny.

"I mean, I feel you on everything you said to Fierce," Carlos added. "But I'm saying, I know the Bruz, or at least I think I know them, and they're not gonna listen to a word you just said. They're only thinking about trying to get some ass, anything beyond the realm of party and bullshit is too far off into the distance for most of them to imagine. It may work while you're here, if that type of thinking works here at all, but as soon as the watchdog falls asleep the foxes are gonna be in the hen house Brother. You can believe that."

"Carlos, Carlos, Carlos. My nay-saying friend, just sit back, I got this, mijo."

THE BUM BRUZ

T hings weren't always all peachy-sunny at the frat house. There was a dark side. My year in the frat house caused a financial crisis in my life that forced me to reinvent myself into the anti-Bruz Bruh that you see now. The biggest cloud that loomed over my life during the frat house era was not pledging, it was being pledged by life for not having a full-time job. Even though President Johnson said that I could return to my post at the college the following fall granted I "stay out of mischief," I was still up a creek without a paddle if I couldn't support myself until then. I was screwed not having my library paycheck to support my education. Not only was I short the income I was making in the library, but I was also forced to pay for my classes out of pocket. That fall, I was barely able to pay for one class with what I had in savings, so I took out a school loan and lived off of the refund I got back from financial aid. Fraternal aspirations aside, I learned that year that my life exists within America, and in America EVERYTHING costs. Money makes the world move around, and without it, my life was at a standstill. College wasn't just some place to go after high school, it was a springboard into the American economy. When I graduated from college I didn't know where I wanted to go, or what I wanted to do. I couldn't go home to my parents because I was a grown man, but Salisbury, NC didn't offer very many opportunities for growth or employment. As an undergrad at Limestone partying and bullshit were the mode of the day, so when I came out, I was still ill prepared to do anything but keep educating myself. I was an English major, so I enrolled in the master's program in African-American literature to buy myself some time. Although it wasn't the most well thought out plan, this was probably the smartest move I made in my young adult life. I now know that a higher education in America is the best launching pad possible to the galaxy of possibilities this world offers. But, like pledging, I had to take my licks before I came to this newfound awareness. When I put all, I'd worked for in jeopardy maintaining an underground pledging network, I was under the complacent assumption that what I was doing was important, and that my career would work itself out as long as I had a job that paid the bills. Now that I was unemployed, the reality of reality sunk in like a rock placed on top of quicksand. I was shopping my resume everywhere and following up on every lead suggested to me, but nothing was coming. I couldn't even get a job bagging groceries at Wal-Mart. I had responsibilities I needed money to take care of, not only for myself, but also to my daughter and her mother. (Child support is a muthafucka!)

I took up extra hours at the group home to make up the slack. I worked 3rd shift because it would give me time to go to class in the mornings and study at night. But at $9.50 per hour, the group home just wasn't enough. After taxes, health insurance, and child support I might have enough money to pay my portion of the house bills, but not much else. On more than one month, I had to let the light bill ride, or ask Ken to float me the money to pay it, which he did (often). I figured I'd make up the shortfall a month or two down the line, somehow. I was good as long as I put something on the bill. Shit, I was hurtin'. I was even more hurt when I found out that the group home I was working for was going out of business for financial mismanagement. I found out only after my last two paychecks from that place bounced. I also found out that during the time I worked at Love First Group Homes, my child support had not been paid by the company a total of seven times. I didn't know that it wasn't being paid because the deduction would show up on my paystub as a debit. Whenever my daughter's mother would call me to tell me that the money hadn't hit her account, I brushed off her call as an attempt to squeeze more money out of me. (As you can tell, we weren't on the greatest of terms.) I tried to call the Child Support office to verify her story, but they always gave me the run around. I learned that year that the Ramsey County Child Support Enforcement Office is not very helpful to fathers. They prefer to only talk to mothers trying to collect money from fathers.

Maybe it was just God showing me some things I needed to see, but at the frat house, my once almost perfect life went from bad to worse in the course of one semester. I went from "creating" a frat house to "needing" to live in the frat house in order to survive. By October of 2004, I was completely out of work. I had almost no savings, no income, and no family to turn to. I was a twenty-eight-year-old adult according to the world, but according to the sum total worth of my life's achievements up until that point, I was still in limbo somewhere between boyhood and a man. My ship was sinking fast, and if I didn't respond quickly, I was going to be swimming up shits creek for dear life. After making a few phone calls, I found myself temporary work. Fortunately, Malcolm Damion, the house manager at Love First, was the Bruz and he got me a job with him at another group home he worked at. This time, I was making $10.00 per hour. But even with the raise, I was still screwed. My child support payments were in arrears for more than four months, so my driver's license got suspended. This meant that I couldn't legally work in the human services field because according to state regulations, "no regular employee can be employed for client care that does not possess a valid N.C. driver's license." Ironically enough, I didn't find this out until I got pulled over by Ralph Young while I was driving to work in the company van. He warned me about my faulty license and let me go at my own risk. Malcolm didn't fire me, but he downgraded my employment status to PRN, which means "as needed." PRN's are excluded from the driver's license rule. True to his word, Malcolm gave me as many hours as possible, and they almost equaled up to a full check, but almost only counts in horseshoes and hand grenades. I managed to juggle my finances for a little while. But by the time Homecoming 2004 rolled around, my pockets were pooped.

"Don't worry about it," said Ken. "I've got the water bill. You just handle your other responsibilities. After Homecoming, I'm sure you'll have a gig lined up somewhere."

"Yeah, I'm sure I will too." I was trying to be optimistic.

"Besides, we've got bigger fish to fry right now. I need you on point this homecoming because you're going to host the Grand Opening of the frat house this weekend." Ken was smiling devilishly.

"Oh, no! That's neo work. I'm gonna be cruisin' and smoozin' this weekend trying to politic my way into a job."

"I told you not to worry about that. Finding a job will take care of itself, if you do your job here at the frat house. There are over two hundred and fifty Bruz who are going to be on this campus this weekend. You don't think one of them will have a job for you? Come on, what do you think the frat's for?" I was still skeptical.

I said, "The frat teaches self-reliance right alongside mutual aid, but some Bruz are iffy when it comes to using discretion about how each should be implemented," hoping he got my point.

"Alright, focus on this weekend, for just this weekend, and I promise that if something good doesn't happen to you by Monday, I will take you looking for jobs myself, as long as it takes you to find a job." He was lying, but his sincerity to his purpose won me over.

The frat house was going to be the epicenter of all the Bruz activities that Homecoming. We planned our whole hospitality itinerary around the place. We were trying to sell the Old Heads and the Grad Chapter Bruz that were visiting on the idea of sponsoring the frat house year-round. All the Bruz talk via the various friendship groupings that they've managed to maintain with one another over the years. So, I knew that I only needed a small cluster of the Old Heads together to lay out my plan to the whole chapter. Once the right Bruz heard the frat house plan, my idea would spread like wildfire, and the Bruz would willingly donate to the cause. My goal was to get the frat house to a point where it ran automatically with or without me. But even without me, at all times the frat house should have been lived in by a mixture of Graduate and Undergraduate Bruz who are charged with the duty of maintaining the house. I even went so far as drawing up a charter and having Carlos and Mudd ratify it by committee. In return for their sponsorship, the frat house would be open to all the Bruz, undergrad and alumni 24/7, or at least as much as feasibly possible. Most of the Old Heads and Grad bruz were pretty well off into their careers, and each had reached a certain level of surplus in their life. Giving a hundred bucks a year to maintain the frat house like it was a timeshare wasn't the most outrageous idea in the world for me to propose, or so I thought. In my mind, I believed that by working together, and giving just a little bit of what we had earned, the Bruz could give back to the school via sponsorship of the house. Sponsoring the frat house would show the Limestone College community and Nationals that Lambda Gamma is truly dedicated to the life-long growth of the chapter, the fraternity, and the Black community.

Me and Ken Simmons agreed that the frat house was supposed to be run like a mentoring program. The house was going to be a space for the older Bruz to invest in the Undergraduates' lives, by providing the chapter space to "live" as the Bruz 24/7. By having a space where the older Bruz and younger Bruz could meet and be themselves, I believed the Bruz at Lambda Gamma could build a bridge that reconnects one of the biggest disconnects facing African-American men today: a lack of communal feeling for one another. Working on the common goal of maintaining a frat house would create a shared existence between men, who by any other means, would probably never speak to each other. The house was going to be symbolic and material proof that it takes Black men working together to build and maintain a community.

Homecoming 2004 was my chance to test my theory in the heat of battle. I decided to run the house like a live- in hospitality room for the weekend. Friday we would have an after five cocktail meet-and-greet at the house before the step-show, and then again at 9:30 pm before the after-party. Saturday, we would tail gate underneath the car port until sundown. Sunday, we would use the house as our remote kitchen for the annual "Goodbye Fish Fry" at the plot. In three days, me, Mudd, Carlos, and the rest of the '04 Bruz transformed Higgins' dusty old house into the Lambda Gamma fraternity house at 1001 Institute St. in Salisbury, NC.

Me, Mudd, and Carlos got along well enough, but Carlos and his LB's stayed in the mix all week, especially Carlos and Preston. The problem was that each one of them had a competing idea of what it meant to be a man and a Bruh at the same time. Carlos thought Preston was weak, and Preston thought Carlos was posing. Drinking always made their emotions spill out onto the side walk. The two were indicative of the lack of understanding that is crippling Black males, leaders and followers.

Tuesday night of homecoming week Preston and Carlos were arguing all through step practice. An hour and a half into rehearsal Carlos blurts out, "If Preston fucks up this step one more time, I'm gonna wreck him." Everyone laughed except Preston. He knew that he wasn't the world's greatest stepper, but he also knew that he was giving it everything he had. It took a lot of courage for a 320 pound man to get on stage and jump around singing for ten minutes. Carlos's ill-placed humor reminded him of the fist fight the two had while they were on line. It was during a moment very similar to this one, and Carlos chose Preston out of everyone to poke fun at. Carlos had a stinging sense of humor, and Preston hated to feel small. So, Preston punched him, and Carlos picked up a chair and threw it at him before the rest of their LB's could break it up. They apologized to each other for necessities sake but bad blood has a way of hiding itself in the nether regions of the body until it is most needed. Preston said, "Very funny, but I'll do you one better. If I fuck up this next step, I'm gonna punch Carlos in the mouth." Everyone broke out into bigger laughter, except for me and Carlos. I had seen too many Bruz fight over too petty of reasons to let this quibble get out of hand. I diffused the conflict between these two by using it to create a teaching moment for all the other Neos.

"Alright y'all, let's get our heads back into the game." I said. "Necessity is the mother of all invention, and crisis is her mid-wife. If we win this step show, the campus is ours for the duration. If we don't win, we might as well fold up our shirts, and go purchase pocket protectors. Carlos, you and Preston arguing is exactly what our haters want us to be doing right now: arguing with ourselves, and tearing ourselves apart. And for what? Because so and so don't like such and such. Psst! That's lame. The time you two are spending arguing about what it is that you don't like about the other one could be better spent working on improving what it is you do like about yourself." I loved the rare moments when I had their complete attention. "We've got a big weekend ahead of us. Winning isn't everything, but it's the only thing we need to be concerned with. In fact, winning is all I want you Neos to concentrate on doing when you graduate from here. This show is a test pattern for your successful journey into adulthood. Wake up the dead when you step. You're marching is symbolic of you marching into your own personal victory in life."

I thought my speech flew right over their heads, but whatever their individual absorption of my words, the Bruz finished step practice without a hitch and went out and killed the step show Friday. The Bruz were so gassed at winning that the after party that followed the show never really quite left the frat house that night. In fact, other than attending the step show and Sunday afternoon fish fry at the plot, I don't ever remember really leaving the frat house that weekend. On Saturday, the tailgate at the house was so crunk that it was pretty much a wrap for me or any of the other Bruz attending the football game. Whenever I did notice anyone strolling across the street to campus, it was usually to get someone who they wanted to bring back to the house.

That weekend, the House played play space for far more personalities than I normally care to deal with. But, that year was the biggest homecoming in Limestone College history. We had over 8,000 attendees; and of this 8,000, at least 200 of them were Bruz from all over the fraternity. The Bruz, and their guests, frequented the house often. There were so many people swarming through the house that weekend that I never got a chance to make my sales pitch to the Bruz. The problem was that we could never get a cluster of just the Bruz together long enough to talk with all the partying that was going on. There were more people at the frat house that weekend than the actual house itself could support. The party spilled out into the street by Friday evening. So, on Saturday, Ralph got two deputies to block off the street, and we turned our tailgate into a block party. The Bruz were in rare form that weekend. We were hitting on all cylinders. We won the step show that Friday night, and the football team won their game that Saturday. So, everybody was celebrating.

Ken Simmons brought enough food to feed an army that weekend, not to mention the fall '99 line brought twenty cases of beer to celebrate their 5th anniversary in the frat. Man, were we drunk. I put the Neo's on grill and garbage patrol, and Mudd was in charge of the kitchen. Among his many other attributes Mudd was something of a chef. Even though we didn't get any business handled that weekend, I still considered the event a major success because we showed the Bruz how much better things could be if we organized ourselves beyond hanging out at the plot for two days once a year. Or so I thought.

The following Monday morning, reviews of the frat house were atrocious. First of all, the inside and the outside of the house looked like absolute shit. When I finally arose from my Sunday night stupor, there were beer bottles, trash bags, and all other types of miscellaneous debris littering the lawn. Even though we kept cleaning as best we could all weekend, there was no place to hold all the trash until collection day. The neighbor across the street, Ms. Johnson, made sure to leave a note on our door to remind us of what lousy neighbors we were. I was also greeted by a hole that Preston and Carlos put in the living room wall after they were wrecking in the house. Preston got mad at Carlos because Carlos told Preston that the girl, he'd brought to the house that weekend as "his girl" was getting nailed in the bathroom by Dirty Red Saturday night after the tailgate. (What can I say, the Bruz are savages) The only reason I woke up at all that Monday morning was a knock on the door by Ralph Young.

"Fierce, I have a warrant for your arrest. You've been charged with running a house of ill repute. I'm gonna have to take you downtown to process you, but you won't have to spend any real time in jail. It's just a business formality." Ralph was as casual about it as a robot.

"So, you say!" I always took offense to legal accusations. "That's a charge. I can't have a record, I've got shit I'm trying to do with my life. I've got to get a job, and an arrest on my record would kill me!"

"Calm down, Fierce. It's not that big of a deal. Your neighbor Ms. Johnson filed for the warrant this morning in response to the other arrest we made this weekend."

"What arrest?"

"Dr. Henry Ford, the English Professor. We had to take him down Saturday evening for groping a minor. He says he was drunk, and doesn't remember exactly what happened, but he's in lock up right now anyways. He was clearly inebriated and could barely speak when we picked him up. But he did say he was coming from here when the alleged incident happened, so that, coupled with Ms. Johnson's complaint were enough for a public nuisance charge. Like I said, it's nothing, apologize to everybody and it will all go away." All I could hear in my mind was President Johnson saying, "stay out of mischief."

"Yeah right, copper," I said. Ralph started laughing. I got dressed and went down to the station. I knew I should have sent Ms. Johnson an extra plate. She was mad because her daughter Gwendolyn, a freshman at Limestone, attended the tailgate with Preston. It wasn't my fault she raised her with loose morals.

Ms. Velma Johnson worked at the school as a UNCF scholarship coordinator. We'd never really had any direct or cross words with one another, so I didn't really get why she hated me and the Bruz so much. When I worked in the library, I always remember our brief exchanges being pleasant. But once I moved across the street from her, Velma became territorial, and standoffish. She constantly spied on the Bruz activities at the frat house, reporting our every movement to anyone who would listen. Mudd always said "she just needs some meat." I thought she was working for the feds because she was so preoccupied with our lives. Dr. Ford's arrest in front of our house, with a frat shirt on, was full confirmation for her of her worst fears. "The Bruz are in that house having SEX." She was constantly running across the street at night to leave notes on our door about our loud music and trash. When we'd go to talk to her about being better neighbors to one another, she would act as if everything were okay. I wasn't surprised I was down at the police station behind some stuff she gassed up, but I was nervous, because I should be working, not perpetuating the system. Ms. Johnson was at the station when I got there. We never got to the booking part though because I got a chance to talk to Ms. Johnson before Ralph started the paperwork.

"Velma, why do you have me down here on this trumped-up charge?"

"Because you need to be taught a lesson Aiden Chance!" Her voice was shriller than a harpy's.

"A lesson? I've got a lesson for you lady. It's a lesson in respect. Mind your own business and tend to your own household."

"I am tending to mines. I know that my daughter was over your house, and I know what you dirty dogs do over there too!"

"Your daughter is grown, and I didn't see anybody dragging her across the street either."

"You never mind about my daughter, Chance." "You brought her up."

"I came to talk to you about what you been doing lately."

"Last I checked I was just living."

"Well, 'living' as you call it just ain't good enough. You need to be trying to live up to your potential, not wasting your time carousing and drinking with your frat brothers. You're better than that. I remember I used to sign your scholarship checks when you were in undergrad. We were proud of you in the grants office back then. You received full tuition aid all four years you were an undergrad. But lately, it seems like you've gone off track. I see you around here all hours of the day and night, hanging out with your frat brothers, not doing much other than tinkering with that place, and I wonder why you aren't out trying to take over the world like everyone else who got some sense nowadays. You got the smarts to be anything you want to be. So why aren't you something? Don't you want to be nobody in life?"

"Of course, I want to be somebody, Ms. Johnson," I shot back. "I am somebody, and I know this. I'm not sure what my life looks like to you, but I can't be concerned with that. What I am concerned with, however, is succeeding in this life on my own terms. That's freedom to me. Or as much of it as this jacked up world will allow."

"Freedom is taking your place in this society, Aiden. That's why you educated yourself, isn't it? If that wasn't your purpose, it should have been, and it still should be. Your generation is unfettered except by its imagination. Break the chains on your brain, and you'll release the shackles on your feet."

When it was all said and done, I got a noise ordinance citation for $50, but no criminal charges. I sent Ms. Johnson over a plate of leftovers via Preston, and her and I were basically on good terms from then on. But I wasn't out of the woods with the frat house just yet. Although my charges were dropped, Dr. Ford's weren't, so I was pretty sure that the school would have something to say about the frat house. Ford was found by police passed out on the frat house lawn at about 10pm on Saturday. To make matters even worse, the local newspaper and TV station picked up the story as soon as it hit the crime blotter, constantly reporting the address of the lawn Ford was found on. Although they didn't report the direct connection between the house and the frat, the implication in every story was that Ford's lewd behavior stemmed from drinking too heavily at a frat party. Headlines reading "Pervert Professor" were all over Salisbury and the surrounding piedmont area. The school made an official statement distancing itself from Ford, but at the same time vowed to "do a thorough internal investigation of the events leading to this incident." The frat used Bradshaw to make a brief statement by the fraternity, disavowing Ford's actions and reports that there was a "frat house" in Salisbury.

Apparently, Ford was accused of touching a young girl inappropriately as she walked past him Saturday afternoon. The official arrest report called it "lewd and lascivious behavior in public." According to the arrest warrant:

> "Dr. Henry Eric Ford, 39, of 5052 Bartholomew Lane, was admittedly intoxicated, on the streets, while attending a fraternity convention on Institute Street. Dr. Ford allegedly groped a young girl's breasts, and smacked her on her buttocks. The

girl's mother, who was a witness to the act, said the 17-year-old was walking along institute street raising money for their church at the time of the incident. Ford was charged with taking indecent liberties with a minor child. He is being held Sunday in the Rowan County jail under a $25,000 bond and is due in court Friday, October 29th."

Basically, Ford was fucked. But I couldn't worry about him because I wasn't in all that great of shape myself. I was still out of a job, and Ford's arrest in front of the house probably wouldn't bode to well with President Johnson. Adding to the mounting public pressure centering around my fraternal ties was the mountain of bills that piled up after Homecoming. The water bill alone for the house during the month of October was $400. Not to mention the light bill, which was $700, and the gas $200. $1300 is not a boat load of money, but when your income is basically zero, it sure seems like it. Added to all of this was the fact that Frank Higgins became shaky about the deal he made with Ken after the whole homecoming debacle came to light.

After reading about Ford's pending trial in the newspapers Mrs. Higgins started a one-woman campaign to rid Salisbury of the frat house, and the Bruz in general, once and for all. According to Frank the ultimatum was given to him that either we leave the frat house, or she would leave their house, with the kids. Not one much for confrontation, Frank cautiously suggested that me, Mudd, and Carlos find new living arrangements as soon as possible. I offered to start paying rent, but he just shook his head "no." Apparently, money was no substitute for peace of mind in his household. "I can hold her off until the end of the semester, but I can't do anything after that."

Admittedly, I can be an asshole at times, but I would never let my life, or lifestyle, intentionally cause another brother strife. That's not what I'm here for. A friend is supposed to multiply your joys, and divide your sorrows. I struck a deal with Higgins, since he obviously wasn't coming to get rid of me of his own volition, I asked him to let us stay at the house until the beginning of next semester, which was three months away, so that Mudd could graduate in December, and Carlos could get a room on campus in January. He agreed to it, reluctantly, but was pleased that he could go home to Regina and tell her how he put his foot down with the Bruz. She thought we ran over his sentimentality for the frat. But really the reason Higgins put up with us was that we were a manifestation of his super ego. If Higgins wasn't so hen- pecked, he would have been right at the frat house with Ford and the rest of us. I know this because I pledged him myself. At age 52, Higgins was the oldest potential I guided through. But he was also the bravest. And the gleam in his eye when he went over wasn't just that of a man who had endured a senseless trauma. It was the look of determination to live the way he chose, at any cost that bereft him. Higgins was out, even though he kept it to himself because he was a school administrator.

Me, Mudd, and Carlos used our time wisely. I used what was left of my school loan refund money to catch up my child support and pay the gas bill plus half the light bill. Mudd earned enough at Little's Church to cover most of the water bill. Carlos started a campus raffle for a new TV and earned enough in one week to pay what was left of the light bill. In two weeks, he raised an additional three hundred dollars. By exam time Carlos raised over $1000 with his raffle idea. The drawing was scheduled for the end of the beginning of December, right after Thanksgiving break. That would be finals week, and the excitement of a lottery drawing would surely generate a crowd looking to blow off steam. They would also be willing to spend money up until the last minute of the drawing to be entered into the contest once they saw the TV Carlos was going to buy with his initial earnings. We muddled through the semester. I got my driver's license back, but it wasn't until December 17th. I also got my 3rd Shift job back, so I wasn't stuck for child support. But I still didn't have a place to live after January. The frat house would have been a great idea if the Bruz would have controlled their lust for partying and focused on building a legacy for the future. Carlos was right the Bruz couldn't get past chasing their own dick, so we'd never be able to play the big game together as a group.

THE MACHINATORS

December is usually the coldest month of the year in North Carolina, but in 2004, mines was at least ten degrees more frigid than everyone else's. After graduation, Mudd and Carlos went home and I was left in Salisbury all by myself. For three weeks I camped out in the cold and lonely frat house. The water got shut off because Mudd didn't pay the bill, and the lights and gas followed shortly thereafter. I worked most nights so I didn't have to stay at the house much. But, without classes to attend, I was at the mercy of the frat house every morning and at least two nights out of the week. Mudd needed to use his last paycheck from Little to move his stuff back to his parent's house in South Carolina, so I was forced to improvise. I got a plumbers wrench from the hardware store, and managed to work up a system of shutting the water back on at night. Storing gallons of it in the refrigerator and around the house, and then shutting it back off in the morning. This worked for two weeks until the water company came and put a lock on the shut off valve. By that time I had enough water stored to sit through an Armageddon. The day after Christmas the lights got shut off because I needed the money for that bill to eat and get to work. Fortunately, Higgins never got his house's additions installed by a licensed electrician, so thirty percent of the house was operating on a separate current than the rest of the house. With thirty percent power, I still had light in the kitchen, the basement, most of the living room, and the carport. Again, fortunately, Malcolm let me cover the holiday hours at the group home so I didn't spend much time at the frat house. When classes started in January, Carlos moved into the dorms, and let me stay with him because he had a single room. This one small act of kindness reminded me that there is a big difference between Frat Brothers and Friends.

— ∞◦∙)◉(∙◦∞ —

"What's wrong Carlos?" I asked.

"The fuckin' Machinators are always machinating, that's what's wrong?" I didn't understand where he was going with this.

"I don't follow."

"Well, you know how you've been staying here in my room since the frat house got shut down."

"Yeah, but it's just until I find a place I can afford." I always had to add that caveat.

"Well, I was at the plot and Preston told me that the Grad Bruz were going to vote on starting a new frat house."

"That's great!" I had been out of the loop of Bruh politics for a minute, voluntarily refusing to attend meetings until I got my financial situation under control.

"Not great! Not great at all. They also want to vote on suspending you from the chapter."

"Suspend me? They can't do that. I didn't do anything."

138

"Well Spears and a few other Bruz are blaming you and your "Out Bruz" mentality for the Ford incident. They say that you're a loose-cannon Bruh, that's why you got fired from Limestone. They also say that if you would have had more control over your house, the public wouldn't have such a negative image of the Bruz in Salisbury."

I burst into laughter, "Ha! Me? I gave a negative image of the Bruz in Salisbury? Please! If anything I made the Bruz hot around here. It's not my fault certain Bruz can't handle the limelight. If you're an administrator at the college, why would you be drinking at a frat party right next door for anyways? Poor judgment on his part. I feel for Ford, but every man has to carry his own cross. And as for Spears and his cronies, I know why they're mad, but I ain't a bit more worried about them than the man in the moon."

"Well, you should be worried about them because they're coming after you with everything they've got. Especially that Spears guy. He has been machinating his little sneaky plots behind the scenes all year trying to get his self onto a public platform to spread his little machinating philosophy. Preston told me that Spears gave a lecture at the leadership conference down in Atlanta over Christmas Break. His lecture was on, "Being the Bruz in the New Millennium." And guess whose picture he flashed up in his power point presentation. Yep, You!"

"What? What the fuck for?"

"According to Spears, you're the prime example of what the Bruz are degenerating into. Hazing obsessed pledge-a-holics."

"That's crazy"

"He cited an article you wrote in Limestone's school newspaper back when you were editor. Something about you supporting pledging coming back above ground." "Man that shit is old. I wrote that my senior year in undergrad. I still feel that way, but how does that make me public enemy number one? I was just expressing a sentiment felt by a lot of Bruz. I was doing what reporters do; conjecturally taking the road less traveled. In the article I said that if the frat stood up for itself, and brought hazing back above ground, the process could run more smoothly, there would be less danger, and we could turn the initiation rite into a teaching opportunity. I got blasted by everybody for writing that article, but I stood by it as the most logical explanation of how to rid ourselves of the hazing lawsuits that threatened to bankrupt the Frat. The Frat thinks we keep getting sued because the Bruz won't stop hazing; I think we keep getting sued because we won't admit that we haze; or rather, that hazing is a part of our organization. If we were upfront about it, we could market ourselves as a dangerous past time, like football. My position takes pressure off of everybody. Plus, hazing in public will diminish the insanely violent atmosphere of unregulated pledging. Who knows…Maybe the Bruz would even stop hazing if pledging was brought back above ground."

"Well, at any rate, Bradshaw is supposed to come and sit in on the next meeting to preside over your impeachment."

"My impeachment?" I scoffed.

"Yeah. It's not called an impeachment hearing, but that's what it is. The Bruz want Bradshaw to sit on a meeting to advise them on how to handle the fallout from the Ford scandal."

"What do they mean 'handle the fallout from the Ford scandal.' There is nothing for them to handle. Support that brother in his time of despair and keep it moving. It could have happened to anyone of us, so I hope we're not meeting to cast judgment on Ford's actions, because none of us are saints."

"Well, you hit it right on the head when you said it could have happened to anyone of us. That's exactly what is bothering a lot of Bruz, especially the ones that were at the frat house during homecoming. Most of them weren't there with their wives."

"Oh yeah, I forgot about that. Jeff Roberts's wife, Carmen, even caught him trying to hunch that one chick Scooter from the band." We started laughing.

"What?"

"Yeah. But she catches him trying to get up on something every homecoming. She ain't really trippin', and neither are any of the other wives. Really. They know who they married, and what type of men they are. Or, at least they should know. I can understand wanting your man to be faithful, but don't blame me or the Bruz for what your marriage is missing. Give that man a reason to stay home."

Carlos was in tears laughing. "Man, you're rough on 'em Fierce. Are you gonna go to the meeting to answer their charges?"

"What charges? This is Bruh politics, it's not a senate confirmation hearing. I'm gonna go in there and tell the Bruz to kiss my ass. I need a job."

"They think that you're a little too over the top with your vision of the frat, and that you willfully created an unsafe environment for the Bruz to be in. The question on the table is whether or not the chapter should formally reprimand or suspend you for illegally creating a frat house."

"What? That's some bullshit."

"I know, but at the last meeting Spears said that you should be charged with improper use of the Fraternities shield and symbols because you never got permission from the governing body of the organization to use the organization's image. And you know that that dude is gonna try to tie hazing in there somehow too."

———••◦❂◦••———

Mines is not to run this train, It's whistle I cannot blow, Mines is not see, how far that this train will go, I am not allowed to let off steam, Or even ring the bell, But let this train go off the track, And we'll see who catches hell…

I remember learning that poem in 1996, two weeks after we first started on line. At the time, I thought I was superior to all of my LB's because I could memorize poems quickly and recite them back flawlessly, even under pressure. I recited this poem to my Dean without effort ten minutes after he'd first given it to us. But the rest of my line was different, they couldn't get the words out right to save their souls. So Slow Jams made me take four licks of wood every time one of my LB's messed up on the poem. After twenty minutes of me getting thrashed, each one of my line brothers learned to say that poem by their self and in unison. I learned a valuable lesson about acting individually in a group setting from this experience. Once again, I was learning a lesson about acting as an individual on behalf of the group.

Chapter meetings are usually boring and predictable. We open with a prayer, then we handle old business, which usually consists of nothing but committee reports and reading the minutes from the last meeting. After that, we handle new business, and then open up the floor for discussion. The email for this particular meeting called for formal attire. The theory is that formal attire will inspire a formal demeanor. On occasions like this the Bruz are usually at their best, smoothly organized, but impersonal as hell. Rather than jokes and familiarity, there

are a lot of handshakes and "good evening, Brothers" passed
around the room. The Bruz don't have formal meeting space,
so we usually use the conference room at Brother Whinette's
used car dealership, or on occasions such as this, rent out the
conference room at the Holiday Inn.

Brother Spears took the floor to address the chapter right
after the PowerPoint presentation on "Aide to Africa" by the
Social Action committee. "Good evening Brothers, we have
a special guest with us tonight. For those of you who haven't
had the pleasure of meeting him already, Brother Raymond
Bradshaw, from Pi Phi chapter in Charlotte is visiting with us
tonight. Brother Bradshaw most recently served the fraternity
in the role of regional intake chairman, and is now our district
representative. We've invited Brother Bradshaw here tonight to
help us preside over an internal conflict the chapter has been
having. As you may already know, one of our chapter brothers
has gotten himself into a spot of trouble recently, and his behavior
has cast a negative shadow on all of us. In the past, I know many
of us have relished the 'bad boy' limelight, but I say that now, in
this day and age, it is time for us as a chapter and organization to
move past demoralizing and degenerate images of ourselves, and
bask in the shekinah light of our glorious tradition that those
greats who came before us fought so desperately to forge for us."

After that last sentence, Dirty Red nudged me in my right
rib to ask me what the word "shekinah" meant. I kept him at
bay with a brief whisper "it's biblical, it means something like
a dwelling place of god or divinity." You could tell that Dirty
Red and the rest of the Bruz, despite their formal attire, were
growing tired of Spears' longwinded monologue. After two more
minutes of unnecessary introduction, I perked up because Spears
mentioned the frat house.

"As you may have heard, Brother Ford said that he got drunk at the frat house. For those few sober-minded Brothers who don't know what the frat house is. It is the personal residence of Brother Aiden Chance and several of the undergraduate Brothers from Limestone College. In my opinion it is a den of iniquity. I don't disagree with the model, but the constituent parts of the so-called 'frat house' are beneath the standards we supposedly pride ourselves on. My question to this body today is what are we going to do about brothers like Chance who go around willy-nilly slapping the frat's name on every hedonistic endeavor they embark upon? Don't we have a right, no, a duty, to guard the fraternity's name against defamation? Shouldn't we check ourselves from within when necessary? Brother Bradshaw, I ask you, in front of all these Brothers, how you would advise us to manage our chapter in the best interest of the fraternity?"

Spears stepped to the side of the podium with a self-congratulatory pause. He knew that every Bruh in the room hated him for saying what he'd said, but he was just as sure that what he'd said needed to be said. And moreover, what he'd said had been on the hearts and lips of the Brothers in attendance but no one was strong enough to say it. "Sometimes you've got to be the asshole Bruh," he told himself.

The entire room rustled in their seats. Awaiting whatever was to come next. I remained unmoved. I knew all eyes were on me, but stared forward with an impassive glare in my eyes. I was oblivious to the doubt that surrounded me. I kept myself calm by mumbling the first stanza of Rudyard Kipling's poem "If".

If you can keep your head when all about you Are losing theirs and blaming it on you;

If you can trust yourself when all men doubt you, But make allowance for their doubting too;

If you can wait and not be tired by waiting, Or, being lied about, don't deal in lies, Or, being hated, don't give way to hating...

Darryl Rivers took the mic. "Peace Brothers, Peace Brothers, Peace. We're not here to level accusations against one another, or continue any personal antagonisms. We're here to do business. No Brother is being charged of anything here tonight. But Brother Bradshaw we did ask you here to advise us on how we should go about maintaining order amongst the graduate and undergraduate chapters. The Ford chase tarnished us all a little bit." Darryl gave a nervous laugh trying to diffuse the tension in the room, but you could tell it was too late. Opinions were forming, sides were being taken, and some where just stepping back waiting to see a good fight.

Brother Bradshaw took the podium. "Brothers, I am honored to be here. Although, I must admit that I am a tad bit confused as to why I am here. Pi Zeta has always been an upstanding chapter within the fraternity, and it saddens me to know that the spirit of brotherhood that has been a hallmark of this stalwart chapter is being tarnished by the individual actions of a few. But like any other organization worth its own salt, Pi Zeta must be tested to show that the love that created it is a love that endures. I know Brothers Ford and Chance personally, and I know that neither one of them intends to do the frat any harm, intentionally, but public mishaps are public mishaps. I'm in no position to tell any man how to act on his personal time, but when you put the fraternity's name on your mission, you step into the world of legal liability. The frat is a business entity as well as a brotherhood. Brothers must remember to separate their personal lives from the fraternity, especially during compromising situations. I served as first vice-grand counselor for the frat in 1992. During that year I defended the fraternity in three cases that could have been easily avoided had the Bruz as individuals just owned up to what they did instead of dragging the frat's name into what they were doing. There are proper channels and protocols that must be followed to create a fraternity house. My suggestion would be to follow those protocols if you men are serious about creating a fraternity house. As for Chance, as I said earlier, I know him intimately he is my granddaughter's father. I know him to be a good man, who is a hard worker, a dedicated father, and terrific frat Brother. We've butt heads together on several occasions, but we were both made wiser for the experience. Brother Spears, if there is something personal between you and Aiden, I'm sure you two intelligent gentle man can find a way to overcome any barriers that might lie between you. As for managing your chapter, I would say work within the rules of the organization to make the organization a shining example of what a group of Black men can do when working together. None of you, however, should take it upon yourselves to 'own' the frat, because none of us do. We lease its image only. And the price that the frat charges us for leasing its glorious image is our humble obedience and pledge to be role model citizens. Is that so hard?" The Bruz burst out into applause.

Darryl Rivers rushed the podium again. "Thank you Brother Bradshaw, inspirational as always! Give Brother

Bradshaw another hand, please. I said earlier that we weren't here to call any brother's out at this meeting, so I only think it's fair that we let Brother Chance have the floor, if he so chooses, to explain his side of the story since Brother Ford is still detained. Brother Chance?"

"Wait, wait, wait!" Brother Spears jumped out of his seat. "Brother Rivers, you said this wasn't going to be a debate, and now you're letting Chance take the floor as if he were campaigning for President."

Darryl quickly interjected, "Well you brought his name up Spears. How would you feel if your name got dragged through the mud and you weren't at least offered the chance for rebuttal?" Everyone shook their heads in agreement. They were still waiting on a fight.

I hadn't expected to speak. But if talking was what the Bruz wanted, I was the least equipped to refuse. I stood up and addressed everybody from my chair for dramatic effect. "Peace Bruz, Peace Brother." Dirty Red and Jeff Roberts nudged me to take the podium. I could feel the indecision of the group as a walked to the lectern. "Good evening," the microphone made that awful squeal that it makes when it gets too close to the receiver. I cleared my throat and spoke again. "Bruz, if I'm here tonight because I've wronged the frat, then I will burn every shirt I own with the fraternity's letters on it right now. But if I haven't committed any real wrong against the frat, then why am I standing before you all defending my character?"

There where whoops and rustling coming from the crowd, "It's alright brother, you're among friends."

"Mines is not to run this train, and its whistle I did not blow, so why am I catching the hell for it running off of the track? I will tell you why…Because life for a Black man is about catching hell and overcoming it."

"Yes Brother!" Someone in the audience shouted. "Brother Bradshaw is right, we should be supporting Brother Ford in his time of need, even if we don't support his actions and are worried about how his public image will affect ours. Since when did any of us become so less than high and mighty that we walked around cowering in fear of what the world thought about us?

The proof has always been in the pudding, and if you are a good man, the goodness of your actions will resonate in your life, despite what your public persona may be. We don't know exactly what happened with Brother Ford, and we're not in the position to cast judgment on him because we don't know the complete details of the case. Our job is to simply pray that the brother has the strength to navigate his way through the rocky seas that are ahead of him. In this past year, I have had my own rocky sea to sail through, and I can tell you all, although I don't have to, that it hasn't been easy. But the troubles that I'm facing today are more than surely going to forge me into the man I want to become tomorrow. Isn't this the lesson that pledging teaches us? I understand that many of you are forced to live austere lifestyles in order to maintain your social position, but that should not come at the cost of sacrificing another brother to the lynch mob of public opinion. As for the frat house and MY behavior explicitly, I dare any one of you to find fault in either one. The frat house was not my thing, it was OUR thing. At no time that I was in that house, did I ever use that place for the sole benefit of me and my lifestyle. In fact, I put my life on hold to create an example of Black male leadership for you Black male leaders. Every organization needs room to grow, and if you can't see that physical space like the frat house is needed to coalesce the undergraduate and graduate chapters' relationship, then I think all of you need to step back for a moment and analyze the purpose of the performative rituals that make up this fraternity. Our founders and the men in the organization who came before us, have endeavored to create a dual-purposed fraternal entity that inspires and promotes, not only group leadership, but also self-leadership. There is a very specific reason that one of the highest ideals we hold ourselves up to is Manhood, not Men-hood, or Group- hood. Brother Spears is right, the Higgins House project was a creation of my own doing and should not be associated with the larger fraternal order in any way. But the foundation that me and the good brothers who cared to labor with me in this act of love with me put down should be used as a template for something greater to take its place. We have the resources before us, gentlemen, to be a turning point in African-American history. The moves we make today can have broad sweeping effects on the generations of Bruz that will inevitably come after—"

"Excuse me Brother Chance," Darryl had to interrupt. "I hate to cut you short, but we're on a tight schedule, and we have drinks and refreshments in back that need to be served. We only rented this room for two hours. Brothers, if there is no more new business to discuss, we can say a prayer and adjourn this meeting."

"Good," heckled Dirty Red from the middle of the audience. "I think that Nigga Chance was high anyways." The whole room burst into laughter. Darryl brought down his gavel four times to restore order. And with that, we closed the meeting in prayer. But I wasn't done. As the Bruz were about to leave, I finished having my say. Before the Bruz could exit their seats, I stood on my chair.

"Peace Bruz! Peace!" I had everyone's undivided attention. For how long, I wasn't sure. "It's good that we got together tonight for drink, to socialize, and swap war stories. But I'd like to start tonight off with a special 'sober toast' to Brother Carlos Ramierez. This young brother has been holding me down in my time of need, and has done everything for me, from setting his dorm room out to me, to sneaking into the cafeteria for food to make sure I eat every day. This Brother exemplifies the type of Brotherhood I think that the fraternity hopes to inspire in all of us. I may be out of order, but I would like to prematurely nominate Brother Ramierez undergraduate of the year."

"Sit your sober toastin' ass down nigga…" Dirty Red.

———◦◦◦▸❮◉❯◂◦◦◦———

"Aw, don't pay the Bruz any mind Fierce, we know you're right about all that stuff." Carlos really was a friend.

"Man, FUCK the Bruz!" We both laughed. "I'm joking, but I'm serious. Manhood not Men-hood. I'm on some other shit from here on out. It's against my nature to live selfishly, but I can't look out for the interests of the group over my own anymore. If the Bruz are caught up in the ways of white folks like everybody else, who am I to argue? If I was a cracker in a suit they'd listen to anything I had to say. But, NO! Because they see a Bruh, who is a Bruh, and doesn't mind being anything other than a Bruh, they're suspicious and dismissive. Like I don't know what the fuck I'm talking about. The other day, Jeff says to me, 'If you knew so much, you'd be gettin' money too.' At first I was mad at him because he was being his normal smart-ass fat self. But then I got thinking about it. That nigga makes a little bit of sense. Fuck it, get money. That's all there is. Or at least that's what's poppin' now. And what's not poppin' is being broke."

"That ain't never been what's up," Carlos added laughing.

"Fuck all these mothafuckas, I'm going to go get my paper. I care, but I don't care. Do y'all's thing Bruz, I'm doing me. I got a kid to feed. This shit is NOT worth going to jail over. The founders did not create these organizations for black men to use them to ruin their lives. I need to work at being a shining example of what the Bruz are, not of what the Bruz will do to maintain the organization. Bruz are gonna miss me. But miss me with that bullshit."

Carlos was choking on his cigarette smoke laughing. "Dawg, you're gonna quit being the Bruz? You can't quit, you're a legend. What will Salisbury Bruz gonna do without you?" I knew he was joking, but his question came from that serious place only a friend knows how to access.

THE PLOT

That last frat meeting helped me finally realize that the Bruz are on a bunch of bullshit. The frat is no better than the Water Buffalo's Lodge on the Flintstones. It is no realer of a force than any of the other haphazardly contrived "Black" organizations that comprise the corpus of "Black Leadership." It's just a bunch of guys getting together to get away from their wives and worldly responsibilities. But that doesn't make the frat unnecessary or trivial. I learned that the problem with the frat wasn't just that the Bruz weren't taking it serious enough. The problem was also that I was taking the frat too seriously. Like a lot of Bruz, I was transposing too many of my personal needs onto the frat. I was asking the frat to produce the type of leaders that I wanted myself to be. The frat just wasn't built for that. Don't get me wrong. The frat is a beautiful thing, and more than that, a very necessary thing. But it ain't the Civitan Club. Sure, the organization aims to build good citizenship by providing volunteer opportunities for its membership, but in practice it doesn't emphasize helping people overcome developmental disabilities. The reason for this is that the membership itself doesn't realize it has developmental disabilities. How could they not be a little fucked up, coming from where most of the Bruz come from. Black America doesn't formally train its leaders or foster them strategically. The frat isn't a training ground for Black leaders but it could be an incubator for them. The rituals and rhetoric of the organization, although geared toward the creation of leaders, are just formalities. The real value in the fraternity comes from the connection to one another that it gives to the rootless people who comprise it. If we aligned the rhetoric of the organization with the reality of the people who take part in it we could consciously raise the next generations of African-American leaders to actually affect change in this flawed society.

Two very interesting things happened to me after that meeting. The first was that I actually got a chance to talk to President Johnson outside the formal confines of work. He actually turned out to be a pretty approachable guy. Normally, he didn't attend frat meetings, but since Bradshaw was in town, he decided to poke his head in, and fellowship with the Bruz before taking Bradshaw to dinner afterwards. He said he was shocked and amazed at my speech. He'd never thought as deeply about the value of the fraternity as I had. He also admitted to entering the meeting with a biased against me and Ford, based on his foggy understanding of the events that led to Dr. Ford's predicament. "You've given me a lot to consider about the both of you, and myself..." he said. He never once mentioned the slightest bit of indignation about me shacking up in the dorms. His silence on the issue gave me the sense that he sort of admired my determination to follow through with my life's goals. He told me to come by his office Monday morning, and we would discuss my future with the college further.

The second interesting thing that happened to me was that I got a chance to ride back to campus with Frank Higgins. I knew who Higgins was as a public figure, but up until that day,

I'd never really gotten a chance to know who Higgins was as a man. On the ride back to campus, he told me a little more about himself and his life story. He'd lived in Salisbury all his life, and he was the youngest of thirteen children. He'd seen the city segregated, and de-segregated. Of all his brothers and sisters, he was the only one that was able to go to college. After graduating the top of his class in high school, he enrolled straight into Limestone to avoid the draft. He wound up enlisting after his junior year though, because he needed a steady paycheck. He came back to Limestone to finish his B.A. after one tour of duty in Vietnam. He tried to pledge the 1978 line, but with work and family, it was an impossible task for him to dedicate his time to college hijinks. At that time, he was a substitute teacher taking night courses at Limestone. Eventually, he earned his B.A. in education and became a licensed teacher at the Rowan elementary. He moved up to assistant principal after receiving his Master's in education administration from Winston-Salem State University. After finally becoming a full principle in 2000, he decided it was time to finish what he'd started almost twenty-five years earlier. He pledged Pi Zeta. He never told his wife what he went through to get through, but he did it because it just seemed like a challenge, he had to overcome in order to feel whole again.

Before Higgins dropped me off at the plot, so Carlos and I could make our way back to Carlos' room for the night, he took us by the old frat house to show us something very special to him.

—∘∘○─⦿─○∘∘—

"Now you two Brothers be careful walking down these basement steps, I don't keep insurance on this house anymore," Higgins joked as he led us down the unlit back steps into the basement.

"Brother Higgins, you ain't brining us down here to show us a dead body you got stored down here, is you?" Carlos joked. I could tell he was praying for a "no" response.

"Naw, I ain't killed anybody since 'Nam......" Higgins was the only one who chuckled. I couldn't tell whether he was laughing because that was a joke, or because the thought of him killing someone in Vietnam tickled his funny bone.

When we got to the basement, he turned on the light. Apparently, the thirty percent lights were just an inherent gift of the house. He walked us over to the storage closet next to the furnace where he kept the mystery boxes under lock and key. He unlocked the door and hoisted each box out one-by-one, and handed them to me, to hand to Carlos, who put them on the floor in the center of the room.

"Let me guess, there's a million dollars stashed in these boxes," I said, trying to take my own stab at deciphering what the contents we were about to lay our eyes on were before the boxes were opened.

"Close, but you're off by a couple of thousand..." Once again, I couldn't tell whether Higgins was serious or playing. He had such a deadpan way of speaking you couldn't distinguish between his humor and his seriousness. His gold-toothed smile didn't help much either. I decided to judge on the side of positive until proven otherwise. "These boxes contain my most valuable memories. I keep them here, and didn't take them home because some memories are best preserved if they can exist outside the confines of your marriage, if you know what I mean." Again, a gold-toothed smile, with no specific inflection.

"I knew it," Carlos exclaimed. "Higgins you were a pimp back in the days!" Now that was funny. We all laughed.

Higgins just chuckled, showing the complete expanse of his gold-grill. "Naw, not a pimp, but I was something like one in my day. I was just a poor country boy from Salisbury, North Carolina." Higgins had the proud drawl that true Salisburians get when they say the word "Salisbury." They all draw it out, to make the sound of the place linger in your ears before you can hear what they're trying to say next. It sounds like Salis-bury.

He opened box number one as he talked, and it was full of old pictures and college memorabilia. "I didn't grow up with money, but I did grow up with a need for it. You see, even though I was the youngest child of all my brothers and sisters, I was also the smartest of all of them too. 'Book Smart' is what my folks used to call it. I was the family's savior on a number of different fronts. But I lost touch with each and every one of my brothers and sisters as I grew up. They all either died young or moved away never to be heard from again really. When I went away to college, even though I was still in Salisbury, I put a million miles of distance between the life I'd known growing up in poverty, and the life I planned to lead as an adult in Salisbury. That meant losing a lot of friends. I made a new family, of my college friends, and kept lifelong companionship with them as best I could. But I only did this because I knew that having distant associates as close friends was the best way to get ahead in this world. Living like this makes you seem social without weighing you down with the burden of truly caring for another person's life. Over the years, it seems that I have estranged myself from the community that I grew up in to get to the community that I live in know. I grew up in this house. My mama left it to me when she died. I never sold it because it was my one last connection to the past. My main reason for buying into you and Ken's plans for this house was because I was hoping that you could help me fulfill a promise that I made a long time ago. A promise to give back to this community."

"Well, that explains a lot," I said. "I knew you weren't doing it for the money." Higgins laughed.

"I most certainly wasn't." He stroked his beard ferociously as he talked. "These white folks ain't givin' up nothin', Fierce. You've gotta sweat, toil, and coon for every blessing that comes your way, Bruh. And I guarantee, there's always somebody hanging over your shoulder trying to sniff out an imposter. You've got to walk like a duck, talk like a duck, and look like a duck at all times, even though they know you ain't one, to get along in this world. I really supported your frat house idea until the Ford thing happened. I had to back off for public's sake. Not only was I looking out for myself, but I was also looking out for my family, the school district, my students, and their families."

"I get it!" I cut him off. "I've lived that story, myself. I know where your train is headed. Just know, I never meant to cause you, or anyone else, any problems."

Higgins' twisted up incredulously. "You didn't cause anyone any harm. Everybody knows Spears blows things out of proportion all the time. You should bring him up on expulsion charges for being so flamboyant." We all started laughing.

"A grown man wearing a scarf in all this North Carolina heat," Carlos added for good measure. "Who does that?"

Higgins opened box number two. It was full of war medals, uniforms, and pictures. "I enlisted for the war to provide a way for me to feed my first daughter. She was born the second semester of my sophomore year. She was so precious, and so tiny, and so free. I wanted to do everything in my power to protect her. But I was broke. No place in this little racist town would hire me either, because I was a Limestone College student. I was a hometown boy too, so word among the wise was that I was getting a little 'too' educated. There was no way I could ever prove it, but it felt like the whole establishment of the city wanted me gone. So, I enlisted in the Army before starting my junior year. I figured I'd do a quick tour of duty, earn enough to pay for college, and provide for my first wife, my kid, and my sick mother. Back then, the Army was considered a good job, even though our kind was usually fighting on the front lines. The pay that a G.I. brought home was way more than I was gonna get pushing a broom at Cone Mill. The racism was also only half as bad. I was scrappy and itchin' for a fight back then anyways, so I went to 'Nam. I was there one day, and the war was over. Ho Chi Min city got toppled, and our attack convoy got turned into an evacuation unit. Ironically, I was stationed underneath one of the Bruz from Lambda Gamma, Edward 'Chief' Manley. He was my platoon leader. When he found out I was from Salisbury, and Limestone, he took me under his wing. I told him that I was going to pledge the Bruz before I left school, but I had a baby, and decided to do a tour of duty first. He told me to never give up on my dreams, and to finish what I started when I got the chance. He said he was going to make sure I got home safely to my little girl. And he kept his word, even though he didn't make it back here himself." Higgins was staring off into space as he talked by this time. I brought him back to life for a second.

"Higgins, I thought you said the war was over by the time you got there? How did Chief die, if you guys weren't really in the war?"

"Whoa. I didn't say I never saw any action. 'Nam wasn't over until it was over. I did spend a month over there, and two years overseas after that. I saw my fair share of carnage. On my last day in actual Vietnam, our platoon was ambushed by a group of Viet-Cong snipers who hadn't got the message that hostilities had ceased. Eddie pushed me out of the line of fire right before being hit in the heart himself by an M-16 shell. As he lay dying, he made me promise to do something special for Limestone College. I also promised to claim his belongings because he didn't have any next of kin back home. I tried to honor his memory when I got back by pledging, but I had to drop. I was twenty-five when I re- enrolled at Limestone and had to work two jobs in two different cities to feed my family. After about a week of pledging I quit because the strain was too much on me. I felt that I had let old Eddie down, until I went through his things, these boxes, one night, reminiscing." Carlos and I were looking at the pictures of Eddie and the other Bruz at the plot.

"Wow, Fierce. These dudes look like they could be us back in the day."

"They were us back in the day," I laughed. It turns out that Frank had a picture of the old frat house and didn't even know it.

"These boxes here saved my life, Fierce." Higgins said stoically. I didn't follow. "Like a lot of Black men back then, Eddie was the type of Bruh who did what he had to do to survive. I didn't know it at the time, but he made me promise to be the custodian of his things because there were items contained inside his belongings that he didn't want anyone, let alone the Army brass, to find." He opened the third box, and in it was a green duffle bag. "I don't know what Eddie was involved in, but I do know that no one walks around Vietnam with a duffle bag full of money." He opened the bag, and it was full of money. "The other two boxes have duffle bags with pretty much the same contents. The bags are full of American, French, Russian, and Vietnamese bills all mixed up. Most of the American money is sorted, but I've never bothered to un-mix the non-American money." I was floored. "I knew I couldn't turn the money in because I'd unwittingly held on to it for so long. Plus, I didn't want to disrespect Eddie's memory. So, I kept the money hidden in these boxes hoping that if I didn't touch it, I'd eventually figure out how to do some good with it." "So, you had all his money in your possession, all these years, and you couldn't figure out what to do with it? You should have told me, I could have helped you out." Carlos joked.

"Well, I didn't say I didn't do anything with it." Higgins added. "I took out $20,000 of it and paid off this house, plus a few bills. I wanted to set up a scholarship fund at the school with the rest, but I didn't want to have to explain to the IRS how I got a quarter million dollars to give away."

"You mean to tell me there is $250,000 in these bags?" I asked.

"Give or take. If you only count the American bills. I don't know the exchange value of the other bills, or if they are still even any good. In fact, I'm not even sure if all of the American bills are still good because I don't know where Eddie got them. Until you guys moved in here and started shifting stuff around, I'd almost forgot that this money was in here. Or better yet, I tried to forget the money was here."

"Once again," Carlos interjected, "I will be more than happy to help you take this money off of your hands and rid your conscience of this awesome burden Brother."

"Well actually, I was hoping that you two would actually help me do just that."

"Don't mind if I do," Carlos started stuffing money into his pockets, but I stopped him.

"Just exactly what type of help are you talking about Higgins. I'm not doing anything illegal for you, or any other Bruh."

"I wouldn't ask you two to. But I do need help destroying all of this money, and judging from your story this evening, I know you two could use it. I trust you because I know you can keep a secret. I'll pay you two

$10,000 apiece from these bills to help me burn it." "That's all we can get?" Carlos was disappointed. "That's all I can give you before you have to report it to the IRS. And trust me, you don't want to report this money to the IRS."

"I'm with it," I said. "But it seems such a shame to let all this bread go to waste like this."

"Well, like I said, I wanted to create a scholarship fund, but it was too risky. The way I look at it, me giving you two ten G's a piece is sort of like a scholarship, and at least I can see the good that the money is doing for myself."

"Who am I to argue with logic like that. C'mon Carlos, we got some work to do, fire up the grill." Higgins went and got us some Charcoal and beers. The three of us sat under the carport burning money for hours. We burned the Vietnamese and Russian money first, because we were sure it was worthless by now. Carlos kept trying to convince me that it wasn't against the law to hold large sums of French money, but I didn't believe him, so we burned all of that next. For fun, we counted up all the American money to see how much we were letting go up in smoke. It was exactly $268, 374.00. I reminded Higgins of how much interest he could have earned if he'd put all that money in the bank over these years.

"Oh, I'm alright financially," he assured me. "My wife is a lawyer, and I'm a Principle. We don't worry too much about paying bills anymore."

"I didn't know your wife was a lawyer. That's why you never told her about the money." Higgins just nodded his head smiling, like we were finally starting to see the light.

I pocketed an extra $7,000 for myself and Carlos says he got thirteen, plus six in French, when Higgins wasn't looking. He told me that he was going to put what he could in the bank and tell everybody that he'd earned the money from his raffle. I convinced Higgins to preserve an extra $100,000 for a project that I was sure would help him live up to his promise to help the community.

"What we'll do with the project cash is start up a scholarship fund through the grad chapter. It has non- profit tax status, so we'll funnel the money through them and give half to the school and put the other half into the bank so the organization will have a bank roll for future years."

"But where are we gonna say we got the money from?" asked Higgins.

"Simple. We'll say that the money came from the sale of this house to an anonymous investor. Federal law doesn't require that buyer a disclose their name during a cash real estate transaction. Higgins you can say that you're donating the money to the scholarship fund to avoid paying capital gains taxes."

"Well, whose name is the house going to go in, if I'm not the owner of record anymore?" Higgins asked. I just smiled.

<hr />

"I'm giving up on hazing, my job in the frat has changed," I told Dirty Red. "You gotta talk to them young boys yourself if you want to know anything about some pledging around here. I'm the advisor, but I am not the Dean anymore. I give them advice when it's necessary, and sign paperwork when it's mandatory, but all that other shit is that other shit. I sympathize with your plight, but I'm just a Griot now. I tell stories to any Bruh who will listen…"

He cut me off in mid-soliloquy. "Yeah, Yeah, Yeah, and there are 8 million stories in the frat, each one is different…"

"…I'm just trying to chronicle as many as I can." "Bullshit, that's what the history book is for…Your job is to make sure these boys go over right. And you the only nigga I trust that works here to make sure that that happens. So, when you gonna start, and who's gonna be over them with you?"

I couldn't help but chuckle to myself over Red's bulldog tenacity about the situation. "Dawg, I'm not getting involved in that, and I suggest that you stay away from that shit too." I pointed to the President's office, which you could see the back of from the plot. "Them niggas in administration are actin' like they're really the feds about that hazing shit nowadays, so I ain't fuckin' wit it. In fact, business is business, and if I find out that there is anything going on but the official process, I have to report it."

"Oh, so LG Bruz don't pledge anymore 'cause you say so, huh?"

"I didn't say that. I merely suggested it."

"That's fucked up, Fierce." Dirty was hot. But I didn't care. I had my sunglasses on and kept staring straight ahead of me as we talked. Dirty Red stood right next to me staring in the opposite direction. This was our way of watching who was watching us as we talked. Presently, I could feel Dirty Red's eyes burning through the side of my skull, but I refused to turn my head to face him. I just kept talking and smiling.

"Not more fucked up than being unemployed; or even worse, a prisoner." I shouldn't have let that last one slip. I forgot who I was talking too for a second.

"Man, fuck jail! One monkey doesn't stop the show.

I'll do the shit myself, if I have to."

"You do that Bruh, and it's you who is doing that. I love you, but the Bruz can't keep going against the frat," and with that, I was through with the conversation, thoroughly upset with myself for missing my midday constitutional.

That one year suspension taught me a lot about life and the frat. For one, the frat is never supposed to be more important than your personal life. If it does become bigger than the rest of your life, you either need to minimize the importance of the frat in your life or step up whatever it is that's going on in your personal life so that all of your energies aren't being wasted in a recreational activity like fraternalism. Although it takes the Brothers in the Brotherhood to keep the organization alive and strong, a major part of the creation of that vitality is the active participation of the members in the organization in making the most of themselves to set an example to the newly initiated and uninitiated alike.

Another thing that I learned during my forced hiatus was that frat brothers and friends aren't necessarily the same things. After I was suspended, rumors about the reasons for, and severity of, my punishment spread throughout both chapters like wildfire. With the exception of Dirty Red, who is always going to be Dirty Red regardless, most of the older Bruz in the grad chapter who were encouraging me to "carry on tradition" scattered like roaches when the lights come on. They were all afraid of being too closely associated with me and "my problems," just in case legal actions were still pending. I can't really blame them though, if I were in their shoes, I would probably try to save my own ass too. Hell, the Fight Club story that resulted in my suspension was me saving my ass. Fortunately, I saved the asses of a lot of other people involved in the process as well. Of the ten undergrads that went over in '04, maybe three are still active in the frat in any capacity other than attending Limestone's homecoming faithfully. Carlos, Mudd and I are still friends though. Carlos even made me the God father of his first son, Stephen. And I was a groomsman at both him and Mudd's weddings.

Hazing and Pledging are such small parts of the frat experience that it almost seems more indecent to talk about them as if they are important to the world, than it does to deny the gory details of this touchy subject to glorify the more friendly aspects of the Black Greek experience. But considering the dangers involved, for everyone involved, and the legal sanctions that can be levied against an offender, I thought it appropriate to share my dearest thoughts about one of my most personal subjects. I'm glad I pledged, and I'm proud to say that I helped men come into the organization the same way I did, but times change, and so too must the methods by which we frat brothers relate to one another. Long live the frat, and death to any evil that divides us.

ABOUT THE AUTHOR

Dr. Armondo Collins holds a PhD in English Rhetoric and Composition, with an emphasis in African- American studies. His literary criticism appears in *The Langston Hughes Review* and *The Handbook of Research on Black Men*. His latest publication "The Media Assault on the Black Male" is an academic companion to this novel. Dr. Collins is currently the Department Head of The Digital Media Commons in Jackson library at the University of North Carolina Greensboro, and an adjunct lecturer with the university's African-American and African Diaspora Studies program.